SHAFTS DRIVEN DEEP

into the Earth's hot core utilized that buried energy to run the world's power station. That broadcast energy alone kept the food factories running. Without those factories and that power, the hungry, overpopulated planet could not survive.

But the cost was high, for the power broadcasts had a terrifying side-effect. While they were on, the human race was unable to stay awake.

Among the rare few with immunity to the sleep compulsion was the astronaut Rafe Arnaul Harald, one of six who had been training on the Moon for the first star voyage. But now, unless humanity could conquer the dark power that was using the sleep phenomenon to paralyze society, that flight might never be made.

To defeat the unknown masters of the sleeping world, Rafe had only the help of a crippled girl, a wolf with a very special ability, and the unique talents of his own mind and body.

Sleepwalker's World

GORDON R. DICKSON

DAW BOOKS, INC.

DONALD A. WOLLHEIM, PUBLISHER

1301 Avenue of the Americas
New York, N. Y.   10019

"You want a soft and easy death, sheep?
    Then go find other graves.
On this hill, men die fighting. . . ."
    (Coruna el Man at the Massacre of Bawnpore)

    "He With Scars" (Dorsai Tales)

FIRST PRINTING, OCTOBER 1972

3 4 5 6 7 8 9 10 11

1

As he stepped through the door into the cosmonaut's gym, the same dry smell of old sweat which the air system could never remove filled Martin Pu-Li's nostrils, and a quarter gravity over Earth normal made his knees bend slightly. The brief case in his hand was suddenly unreasonably heavy. He straightened knees, back, and shoulders against the pull of the artificial gravity. He was no cosmonaut, but at forty-three he was still tall and athletic as ordinary men went—and it was only a quarter extra weight.

At the far end of the gym Rafe Harald was swarming up the climbing rope, using only his arms. Even with his sweat shirt off and his muscles standing out against the effort, his body did not look remarkable. The body of a systems programmer who played a fair amount of handball, perhaps. Martin walked to the foot of the rope.

"Rafe," he said.

Rafe glanced down from the top of the rope at the ceiling.

"Step back off the mat," he said.

Martin took two steps backward from the gym mat that was positioned under the bottom end of the climbing rope. There was something like a gasp of air past his face and a jarring thud at his feet. Rafe lay on the mat on his back, smiling, legs together, arms spread wide, palms down on the mat like a child about to make angels in a snowbank.

"What kind of a fool trick's that," said Martin, angry without thinking, "in one and a quarter gravities?"

Rafe sat up and got easily to his feet without using his hands. He did not do it like someone who does an exercise. He did it absent-mindedly, as the most convenient way of coming to a standing position from where he was.

"No danger," he said. "Try a slow-motion camera on

me at impact sometime. Toes, ankles, knees, hips—roll backward and slap down with both hands like the villain taking a stage fall in an old-fashioned melodrama."

"Yes, yes," said Martin impatiently, glancing at his thumbclock. "The shuttle's waiting for me. What was it you wanted?"

"You," said Rafe gently.

He looked directly into the eyes of Martin, and Martin, suddenly reminded of the fact that he was hunching once more under the extra gravity, straightened to his full six feet two, so that he had at least two inches on Rafe.

"Well, I'm here," he said. "What was it you wanted to see me about? And why did it have to be here, anyway?"

"Here, because no one ever comes here any more—not even my three fellow cosmos," said Rafe. "And I wanted to see you so I could take over your brief case and some of your other things. I'm going down to Earth." Under the brown, momentarily tousled hair, his light-blue eyes looked out of a pleasant narrow face with a coldness new to Martin. Rafael Arnoul Harald looked less like a hand-ball-minded programmer now than Martin had ever seen him look before. "You don't think I'm serious?"

"Or else you've gone crazy!" Martin's voice, a politician's voice, came closer to sputtering than it had since he had been six years old. "You don't think I'm going to let one of our cosmonauts risk himself back down on Earth? The four of you represent a trillion-dollar investment—let alone all the hopes of the Project."

"I'll take your brief case." Rafe held out a hand. The other man hesitated, and a little extra gentleness came into Rafe's voice. "Come on, Martin. You don't want me to have to take it away from you."

Wordlessly, Martin passed the brief case into Rafe's lean hands.

"Unlock it," said Rafe. Martin fished in his pocket for the small silver key and complied. Rafe folded the cover back. "Now, empty your pockets into it, wherever there's room."

Slowly, Martin brought from his various pockets, pen, pencil, pocket calculator, handkerchief, credit book, card holder—all the little impedimenta of a man about to go on a journey. Rafe accepted them into the open brief case.

"Cash?" Rafe asked when Martin finally stopped

digging. The Project Head smiled sourly and reached into a hip pocket to produce a wallet and a handful of coin tabs.

"Thought of that, too, did you?" he said.

"I've only been on the Moon four years," said Rafe. "I remember a few things." He nodded across the bare gym floor to a brown metal equipment locker. "Over there. I'll lock you up in that. Don't worry. There's a chair inside— even something for you to eat and drink—and plenty of air circulates through it. You won't be locked up more than about nine hours."

They were already moving across the room toward the locker.

"What good do you think this is all going to do you?" asked Martin over his shoulder. "The shuttle's waiting for me. The captain hasn't any orders to take you to Earth, instead."

"He hasn't any orders not to," said Rafe. "Keep moving, Martin." Ahead of him the wide-shouldered back of the Project Head was stiff with resentment. Rafe put a hand softly on one blue-velvet-jacketed shoulder and urged the other man forward until they came to the locker itself.

"Open the right-hand door," said Rafe. "And pass me out the suit and other things you'll find on some hangers inside there."

Martin obeyed.

"My God!" he said. For the first time there was something like fear in his voice. "You're actually going to do it. You've gone off the deep end. You're psychotic!"

"You know better," said Rafe. "Into the locker. Now, sit down." He was already stripping off his gym clothes and dressing himself in the street apparel he had not worn since coming up from Earth four years ago, December fourteenth.

Martin turned around and sat down. His face was twisted.

"At least give me an explanation," he said. "You can do that if there's any sense to all this! Don't you realize whatever you're doing could be something that could give the Project a bad name? It could be the last straw in cutting off our appropriations entirely. Earth's already wound up because we haven't sent a man out interstellar before this!"

"Earth and most of the people up here, Martin," said Rafe.

The yellow skin of Martin's face tightened.

"You're accusing me of something?"

"Maybe," said Rafe. "You, or possibly Pao Gallot, or Bill Forebringer."

Martin stared at him, tight-faced.

"That's right," said Rafe, knotting his cravat. "One of you three has to be involved in whatever it is. Together, you run the Earth—and the Project, too."

"You *are* crazy!" said Martin. "None of us wants to run anything! Pao lives and dies for the Core Tap stations. Forebringer's the UN Marshal, nothing more. And I—I've given my life to the Project out here to get to the far stars!"

"And every four months the three of you get together down on Earth and decide how the world's to run until you meet again," said Rafe.

Martin stared. Then, slowly, he began to shake his head.

"I can't understand it," he said. "I'd have sworn of all four cosmos you were the most stable."

"Was—and still am," said Rafe. "You still don't understand? I'll give you a name, the same one I'm going to be giving Pao and Forebringer as soon as I touch down on Earth and see them. Ab Leesing."

"Ab . . . who?" Martin frowned.

"Abner Carmody Leesing," said Rafe.

Martin shook his head.

"I never heard it before."

"I just called down to Earth yesterday. He's been missing for eight days. Did one of you have him picked up?"

"I tell you I don't know who you're talking about!"

"Come on, Martin," said Rafe. "There aren't any ordinary people up here on the Project. And you're one of the most unordinary of us all. You heard the name once upon a time, and so you can remember it again if you really want to. Make the effort."

Martin frowned darkly, but for a second his eyes became absent, thoughtful, then clear.

"Abner Carmody Leesing," he said. "A biophysicist. You recommended him yourself for the Project, three years ago. A screening committee decided against using him."

He stared at Rafe.

"I didn't have anything to do with it," he said. "If the committee recommends against a man, I've got to follow that recommendation. You're blaming me?"

"You—or somebody. I had a look at the files yesterday afternoon."

"*My* files?" Martin's dark eyes went opaque, almost muddy.

"The committee minutes in the Ab Leesing case," said Rafe, buttoning the three ivory buttons of a maroon swallow-tailed jacket at his narrow waist. Dressed up, he looked a little like the character on the label of an old-fashioned Johnnie Walker Scotch Whisky bottle. "There wasn't anything there to make a Congressional case out of. Just two members with their own axes to grind. Only four other men who'd rather play safe than take risks. Only a concentration on details that didn't count and a total avoidance of the real potentialities of Ab's work."

"Proving what? What did we need with another bio-physicist?"

"The cryonics approach has failed on the Project, hasn't it?" said Rafe. "What do you think?—Sit tight, Martin. They'll be letting you out in about nine hours."

He closed the one open door of the cabinet, and metal clashed on metal loudly in the silence of the gym. Inside the cabinet Martin said something, but Rafe, already turning away, did not catch the meaning of the words.

He went quickly across the gym and out of the door Martin had entered a few minutes before. In the white-painted metal corridor outside he turned right and went along it until a door let him through into a carpeted section of corridor with imitation wood paneling. It was a short cut through the cosmonauts' section of Project Far Star, Moonbase—the closest thing to luxury off Earth, almost a small apartment apiece for the four of them. One of the apartment doors was open, and Mary Vail came out, wrapped in music—Sibelius—from a player in her room.

Unlike Tannina Or, the other woman among the four cosmonauts, Mary was one of those people who could drug herself on music. She had become good at it, particularly this last year. Now she stopped in the doorway of her room, staring at the way he was dressed—a slight, dark-haired girl with golden eyes.

"You're going to Earth?" she said.

"On the shuttle." He stopped for a moment to face her. "While Martin stays locked up in the gym. Would you kind of help to keep people clear of the place for the next nine hours?"

She nodded. Suddenly she threw her arms around him and clung to him like a child.

"Do something!" she said, her voice muffled against his chest. "Do *something*."

"I'll try," he said.

He held her and gently patted the dark crown of her head. It was strange. They did not love each other, but after four years of the four of them being set apart and together like this, they did not *not-love* each other, either. He could feel the unhappiness in her through his arms, and for a second there it was—all the agony of a world in one small body. He sensed the movement deep within, the near-telepathic empathic gut-feeling that had always been a talent in him. Suddenly, he was as aware of how Mary Vail felt as if he were Mary herself.

She let him go and stood back into her doorway and the sound of her music.

"I'll watch the gym," she said. "Be careful."

He nodded.

"Absolutely," he said, and went on down the corridor, past the other three closed doors, one of which was his own, and through a farther air-lock door into the staging area with its bare metal walls, racked crates, and general warehouse appearance.

At the far end of the staging area was the tunnel entrance to the shuttle. Up at the end of the tunnel, in the open air lock of the shuttle itself, Peer Wallace, one of the crewmen, stood negligent and somewhat sour-faced guard. He brightened at the sight of Rafe.

"Hi, Peer," said Rafe, ducking his head under the low, curved upper rim of the air lock. The sound of the pressure-gradient air pump, deliberately noisy for safety's sake, hammered in their ears and made him raise his voice. "Where's Charlie?"

"Up front," said Peer. "Better hurry, though. We're all checked out and on stand-by, just waiting on P-for-Perfect." He stared curiously at Rafe's clothes. "You're going down with us too?"

"I'll let Charlie explain it," said Rafe. He turned and went up the connecting corridor, so narrow he almost needed to walk sideways, and rapped with his knuckles on the half-open air-lock door to the pilot room.

Inside the pilot room one of the command chairs was empty. In the other was a heavy-bodied, hook-nosed man with the graying stubble of a very short haircut on his round skull. He was wearing navy captain's blues. He spun the chair around to face Rafe at the sound of the knock.

"Rafe!" he said, and smiled. "Well, what's this? You joining us for the trip down?"

"That's right," said Rafe. He turned, put his hand on the edge of the air-lock door, but could not budge it. "How do you close this thing?"

Charlie Purcell reached behind himself without looking and touched a button on a control panel. The air-lock door swung silently closed.

"What is it?" Charlie asked, looking keenly at Rafe. "Something special?"

"Yes," said Rafe. "You're sure your intercom and everything like that's off? All right. I've got a special package here." He patted the brief case he held with his free hand.

Charlie's face brightened suddenly. His eyes fastened on the brief case.

"A break-through?" he said. His voice was abruptly a little hoarse. "At last—finally they've licked the freezing problem?"

Rafe shook his head.

"I can't tell you," he said. "But I'm taking it down instead of Martin—for good reasons. He won't be going this trip. You take me instead."

"But why?" Charlie stared.

"Can't tell you that either, sorry," said Rafe. "There are reasons for doing this different from what you'd think. There's no order cut for me to go down. Nothing. Martin's sitting in a locker in the cosmos' gym—with a chair, something to eat and drink, and Mary Vail to stand watch. Only Mary, you, and I know about this."

"God in heaven!" said Charlie, his face still alight. Then some of the illumination went out of it. "But what'll I tell the rest of the shuttle crew?"

"Just tell them Martin sent me in his place for reasons that can't be explained," Rafe said. He smiled, inviting Charlie to smile back at him. Few people could resist him when he smiled. Charlie grinned back now. "Of course, if they want to go ahead and guess, we can't stop them. But warn them not to say anything after we've landed on Earth."

"Don't worry!" Charlie swung energetically back to his controls. "You can trust this crew."

He began to talk over the intercom. Rafe turned and carried the brief case back down the corridor, off along a side corridor, and through an air-lock door into the passenger section—a round room in the belly of the shuttle with several rows of overstuffed chair seats, three abreast. He chose one. Outside the thick glass of the passenger section's window, he had a view of a slice of the daylight Moon surface, with the black, star-pricked backdrop of space beyond. Earth was not in view from this angle.

A second later a red warning light shone from the ceiling, there was a slight tremor, and the Moon slice began to rotate away below him. The shuttle had lifted from the moon.

Rafe opened the brief case and skimmed through its contents, but he found nothing important. He relocked the case and settled himself back in his chair. Long ago, as a twelve-year-old, he had taught himself to take sleep under any and all conditions, when the opportunity presented itself. He closed his eyes now and slept.

He woke to a touch on his shoulder.

"We're down, Rafe," said the voice of Peer Wallace. Rafe blinked at the yellow-bright, early afternoon light of Earth's surface, coming in through the window. "We're in the cradle at Armstrong Field, Oregon. There's a limo and people waiting for you—for our Project Head, that is."

Rafe nodded, yawned, stretched, and got to his feet. He followed Peer out of the shuttle, stepping a little clumsily. Even for him, four and a half hours of sleeping upright in a chair had its stiffening effect on the body muscles.

Outside the entrance air lock now was a forty-foot metal ladder leading to the ground. At the foot of the ladder was a black, two-wheeled limousine, with a driver behind the control stick in the front compartment and the door to the rear compartment open. Outside the door stood an obvious secret service man and a slim, blond woman in her early thirties.

Rafe went down the steps to them, and the woman met him as he stepped off the last one. She was frowning.

"What's this?" she said. "Mr. Pu-Li didn't say anything about one of the cosmonauts coming down in his place."

"Exactly," answered Rafe. "It wouldn't have worked if people had known." He smiled at her, but she was one of those who could resist him. Her face remained cold.

He walked past her and got into the rear compartment of the limo. Within, it was dark after the shuttle and the daylight, and the seats felt abnormally overpadded under Earth gravity. After a second's hesitation she got in herself and sat down beside him. She spoke to the glass panel separating them from the driver, who had now been joined by the secret service man. The gyros of the limo hummed as the vehicle lifted and balanced on its two wheels, fore and aft, and began to move off across the concrete landing area toward a roadway at its edge.

"How long before we get to wherever I'm meeting the other two gentlemen?" Rafe asked.

"Why would you need to know?" Her voice was suspicious, almost hostile.

"Because," he said patiently, turning to look directly into her face, "time may be vital right at the moment."

He continued to hold her eyes with his own. After a long second, she looked away.

"About half an hour," she said. "They're just outside Seattle."

She sat back in her seat, staring straight ahead and giving him her profile. For her age and in spite of the severity of her expression, she had a pretty face except for the dark circles under her eyes. Once more he felt the gut-sensation of response to a witnessed suffering.

Probably she dreamed too much, Rafe thought. Most people on Earth dreamed more than they wanted to, nowadays.

2

They spoke only once more on the half-hour trip.

"You evidently know me," said Rafe gently, after they had left Armstrong Field behind them and were rolling along the freeway through the spring-green countryside with the limo's spoilers extended to keep them from becoming airborne at a hundred and eighty miles per hour. "But you didn't tell me your name."

"Lee," she said.

There was something hopeless about the way she answered with a single name only—as if she had accepted the unimportance of being no more than a factotum or a pet animal. Rafe turned his gaze back to the ribbon of concrete that was the high-speed lane, extending itself endlessly before them. He said no more until they ended their journey.

The end came after they had left the freeway and turned in, some distance down an asphalt road, at the gate to what looked like either a very large private home or a small institution. The gate area and the grounds were scattered with men and women in clothes of civilian colors, but wearing the same professional aura as the secret service man in the limo's front compartment.

"Here?" said Rafe, as the limo pulled up before a large front door.

"We'll go right in," Lee answered. She got out of the car and he followed her.

They were let through the front door and met inside by two more secret service men types.

"Just a moment, please," said Lee. "Wait here."

She went ahead down a carpeted hallway with a wide stairway rising from it. Past the foot of the stairway she knocked at a white-painted door and entered. After a moment she came back.

"This way, Mr. Harald," she said.

Rafe followed her, holding the brief case and followed by the two men. At the door Lee stopped and turned to him.

"The brief case, please?" she asked, holding out her hand. Rafe smiled and gave it to her.

She passed it to one of the men, who backed off with it. The other man followed Lee and Rafe into the room.

It was a library, or a study of sorts. Seated in large armchairs flanking a fieldstone fireplace in which paper, kindling, and logs were laid but not lit were the two men with whom Martin Pu-Li had had an appointment this morning. It was not hard for Rafe to recognize them.

Willet Forebringer, the Marshal appointed by the United Nations to hold extraordinary powers over all the world's police forces as long as the emergency created by the soporific effect of the broadcast power from the Core Tap units continued, was a thin, stiff-backed man in his fifties. The black silk solitaire he wore about his neck instead of a cravat emphasized the white boniness of his face above, with its gray hair clubbed at the back of his head and gray eyebrows. Pao Gallot, seated opposite Forebringer, was sixty and looked forty, with a close cap of perfectly black hair and a round, hard body under a round, inoffensive-looking face. Neither of these two evoked the empathy response in Rafe. Of the two men, Forebringer was by far the man most likely-looking to begin an interrogation, but in fact it was Pao Gallot who spoke first—in English, but with a slightly hissing French accent.

"I take for granted," he said, "you brought some kind of authorization from Martin Pu-Li."

Rafe shook his head. He looked at Lee and the man who had accompanied them into the room. Pao also looked at the man.

"Did you search him?" the Chairman of the Core Tap Project asked.

"No, sir. He's one of the cosmo—"

"Search him now," said Forebringer. The man came forward almost apologetically and ran his hands over Rafe's body. Rafe smiled at him, reassuringly. Behind them there was a rap on the door. Lee turned and went to it—to return carrying the brief case.

"He's all right," said the man.

"This is all right too," said Lee.

"Give it to him, then," said Pao. "And wait outside, both of you."

Lee and the man obeyed. As the door shut behind him Rafe walked forward with the brief case under his arm and took a chair facing the other two men.

"We didn't ask you to sit down, Harald," said Forebringer. "You know you've made yourself liable to arrest, showing up here? None of you on the Moon Project had authority to return to Earth, except Martin."

"Where is Martin?" asked Pao Gallot.

"Back on the Moon," said Rafe.

"He sent you, did he?"

"No," said Rafe. "I locked him up and took his place."

"And the shuttle brought you down without orders?" broke in Forebringer.

"I let them think I was carrying word of a breakthrough—a solution finally to the problem of nerve decay under the freezing process that's been holding back the Project from its first Star shoot for nearly three years now," Rafe said. "I let them think there were secret reasons why I had to bring Earth the news about it, without authorization, instead of Martin bringing it."

"There isn't any such solution, is there?" Pao asked.

"No," said Rafe.

"I see." Pao hesitated for a moment. "Then you'd better tell us why you're here, hadn't you?"

"Abner Carmody Leesing," said Rafe. "A biophysicist I recommended for work on the Project three years ago, only a committee decided against him. I phoned down to Earth yesterday, Moon time, and couldn't get him. I was told he disappeared eight days ago."

He paused and sat looking at the other two men.

"Well?" demanded Forebringer after a minute. "What about this—this Leesing?"

"That's what I asked Martin," Rafe said. "Before I locked him up and took his place on the shuttle. He claimed he didn't know anything about Ab's disappearance."

Forebringer looked at Pao. Pao lifted his dark eyebrows, looking back.

"Are we supposed to know?" demanded Forebringer. "Is that it?"

"One of you two—or Martin," Rafe said, looking from

one to the other of them. "Maybe two or even all three of you."

"What the *hell*"—Forebringer came down hard on the last word—"do you think? We've got time to keep track of every missing person in the world? We've got a world to run."

"A world to bury," said Rafe softly.

High in the chimney above the fireplace a little afternoon wind moaned softly. A breath of air came from the fireplace itself, bearing the invisible odor of old, charred wood and unswept ashes.

"What's that supposed to mean?" It was Pao Gallot.

"You know," said Rafe unsparingly. "Did you think you could put a handful of the best minds of the generation off in a corner on the Moon with nothing to do but think, and not have them figure out a good deal of what was going on? Three years now, the Moonbase Far-Star Project's been stuck dead on the problem of nerve damage under the cryonics process. Without cryonic suspended animation, there's no point in trying to send a ship even as far as Alpha Centauri. Meanwhile Earth's dying."

"Dying?" Pao bristled. "No one goes hungry nowadays. No one. And with the Core Taps powering the food manufactories we can hold out a thousand years—let alone until you lick some little freezing problem."

"Dying," repeated Rafe. "Man doesn't live by bread alone. That woman who brought me here's half dead already. So are people on the Project, back on the Moon. But that's not what bothers me. One of you, two of you, three of you, maybe, are deliberately letting it die."

Pao grunted.

"You're psychotic," said Forebringer between tight lips.

"That's what Martin said to me," answered Rafe. "And he knew it wasn't so when he said it. You know it's not true yourself. If any two men know, you both know the world's dying. And for some reason, even if you're not actively helping the process, you're choosing to let it die, rather than fight the situation. What is it you're afraid to fight?"

"Judas Priest!" said Forebringer to Pao. "Let's not listen to this."

"Another moment or two," said Pao, lifting a square

hand slightly from the knee of his plum-colored half-pants. "What's the point, Harald?"

"I told you," Rafe said. "I want to know where Ab Leesing's gone, and who's taken him."

"But not why?" Pao leaned forward a little, and his blue jacket creased over his belly.

"I know why. I think you do, too." Rafe looked steadily back at him. "Ab's work must have come up with something that would break the deadlock on the Project. So picking him up's going one step further. Not just sitting back and letting the world die, but taking steps to make sure it does. Which one of you made him disappear?"

"Not I," said Pao, sitting back in his chair. "I don't have time for anything but the Core Taps and the food factories. In fact, my job's gradually wrecking me." He looked over at Forebringer. "Bill?"

Forebringer's white face was ugly.

"I don't have to dignify questions like that with answers," he said.

"You're saying no, too," Rafe said. "And one or both of you're lying."

He looked at them. Both men moved restlessly. Forebringer put his arms on the padded arms of his chair as if to push himself to his feet.

"All right," said Rafe. "You're ready to quit talking. Let me show you something first. Could I have one of your men from outside the door there come in so I can demonstrate something for you?"

"Demonstrate what?" asked Forebringer.

"Just let me show it to you first, before I get into any explanations," Rafe answered.

They hesitated.

"This man," said Pao. "Your demonstration won't—you don't plan on harming him?"

"Does it matter?" asked Rafe.

"No," said Forebringer sharply, before Pao could speak again. He pressed a button on the base of a phone standing on a table beside his chair, then picked up the phone.

"Send Jim in," he said.

Behind Rafe the door opened. Rafe got to his feet and went to meet the secret service man who stepped into the room, closing the door behind him.

"This way," said Rafe, taking him by the elbow as they came face to face. "We need you over here—"

As he spoke, he braced himself against his own reluctance to hurt, and dug the stiffened fingers of his free hand up under the breastbone of the man. The other collapsed upon him. Rafe caught and held him upright with the hand that had originally taken him by the elbow. Rafe's other hand slid in between the man's coat and waistcoat to come out with a palm-sized pill-gun. He slipped the gun into the waistband of his own pants and half dragged, half carried the other man to the chair in which he himself had been sitting earlier. He lowered the unconscious body into the chair.

"What happened?" It was Pao Gallot. Both the other men were on their feet now, watching him.

"You didn't see?" Rafe asked. "My reflexes are pretty fast, of course."

He turned around to face them, drawing the pill-gun.

"Sit down again," he said.

They stared at the gun and sat.

"Good," said Rafe. "Now, as I said, my reflexes are pretty fast. Fast enough that I can put the gun back in my pocket and use both hands to tie this man up—and still reach the gun again in time to shoot you both if you start to move out of your chairs or make any noise. You understand?"

"Mr. Harald—" began Pao, almost soothingly.

"No noise. No talk," said Rafe. Pao closed his lips. Rafe put the gun back into the waistband of his trousers.

He walked around behind the chair in which the unconscious man lay sprawled. Taking the man's cravat off, he gagged the slack mouth; then pulling the limp figure to the floor, he unthreaded the lacings from the man's boots and with these tied wrists and ankles together behind the unconscious back. When the man was completely trussed, Rafe dragged the body out of sight behind one of the couches in the room.

"Now," he said, turning back to Pao and Forebringer. "You two and I are going to leave in the limo that brought me here. Tell them outside no one is to come into this room until further orders. We'll take along Lee to drive the limo for us—no one else. You understand?" They nodded. "Up on your feet, then, and go ahead of me out of the door. Think up what you need to say yourselves, and don't forget I have the gun. I doubt that anyone you have here can kill me quickly enough so that I can't kill the two of you. Here we go."

They walked to the door and out into the hall.

"Lee," said Forebringer. "Come along. This room's to be sealed until further orders. Mr. Harald, Mr. Gallot, and myself have someplace to go. You'll drive a limo for us— no one else is going."

"Yes, sir," she said. "The limo that brought Mr. Harald's still out front. Do you want to take that?"

"That's fine," said Forebringer.

They followed her down the hall, Rafe walking just behind the other two men. The outside air was still cool and fresh on their faces as they got into the limo—the three men in back, Lee in the front compartment. She took the stick in her hand, and the vehicle rose smoothly on its two wheels and curved around the driveway out onto the asphalt road.

"Where to, sir?" It was Lee's emotionless voice through the speaker connecting the front and rear compartments. Forebringer glanced at Rafe.

"I guess, Armstrong Field. Where I came in," Rafe said. "Unless you can think of someplace closer where we could get a three-place-or-better VTL aircraft?"

"Armstrong Field, Lee," said Forebringer. He leaned forward and turned to "off" position a switch among the controls below the small grille in the compartment's forward wall, from which Lee's voice had come. "Lee can't fly a vertical take-off-and-landing craft."

"I can," said Rafe.

Once again the ride was a silent one. It was not until their limo was turning back onto the roadway that ran down one side of the landing field itself that Rafe spoke up once more.

"Now," he said to Forebringer. "Order that three-place craft. Tell them it's an emergency—or anything else you want. But they're to find us one right away. We'll take anything that's ready to fly, up to commuter bus size."

Forebringer reached for the controls under the grille and punched out a call number.

"Terminal Police," said a voice from the grille.

"This is Willet Forebringer. Reference code Ajax Ten. I need a three-place VTL immediately for an unspecified destination. We're at the edge of the field now. Can you have it ready for us by the time we reach your office?"

"Sir—I—" the voice rattled in the speaker, almost stammering, "Mr. Forebringer, maybe you'd better talk to the captain here, sir. I'm just a desk patrolman—"

"You'll do," said Forebringer grimly. "Just relay the order—and it is an order. Now, tell me, can you have the VTL ready?"

"Sir—I don't know, sir—"

Forebringer cut off the phone connection sharply. He sat back, looking at Rafe.

"What's wrong with me?" Forebringer said, sourly. "You'd think I wanted to go on this trip."

"If you're an honest man, maybe you do," said Rafe softly.

They followed the road around past the tall buildings of the ordinary terminal, to a smaller building with glowing yellow letters spelling out POLICE in the air above it.

"We'll stay in the car," Rafe said, "right up until we board the aircraft. Speak to them again, Forebringer."

Forebringer leaned forward and used the phone connection once more. They were told that a five-place ship was ready for them on the landing pad on the far side of the building, and they drove around to it.

Five minutes later, with Rafe at the controls, but with his eyes focused on the mirror showing Pao and Forebringer seated behind him with their hands carefully in view in their laps, the VTL leaped directly skyward from the landing pad, and the foreshortened figure of Lee dwindled away below them.

At an altitude of seven thousand feet, Rafe entered the traffic pattern above the field, and came out of it a minute or two later, headed due east. He lifted to eighty thousand feet, put the controls on auto, and swung his seat around on its gimbals to face Forebringer and Pao.

"Is it too much to ask where you're taking us?" Pao said.

"I'm not sure," Rafe said. "We'll just head east until it gets dark or the two of you fall asleep."

Both the other men stiffened.

"You damn fool!" Forebringer said. "Don't you know any airfield we pass over on automatic pilot will try to pull us in unless there's someone awake at the controls to cut us out of the traffic pattern? And a ship this size hasn't the response mechs to get itself landed by airport control?

You fly us into a broadcast area and we'll end up a pile of junk on some landing pad—"

He broke off abruptly. His eyes narrowed, staring at Rafe.

"Or maybe you're figuring on not going all the way asleep," he said. "What are you? Some sort of zombie?"

"You could say that," answered Rafe.

He expected one or the other of them to question him further after his saying that. But neither did. Pao sat as he was. Forebringer leaned back in his seat and folded his arms across his chest like a man who has come to a decision.

3

"I don't know what ability you think you have in resisting the soporific effect," said Pao, some little while later. "But if you know anything about those who can resist it, you know that no two people react alike. Now, it's over four years since you were on Earth, and at that time the first Core Tap hadn't been set up to broadcast power to the food manufactories. In short, you haven't had any actual experience with the way you'll react to broadcast power—"

"I visited one of the experimental stations two years before I went to the Moon," said Rafe.

Pao closed his mouth and sighed slightly. Below the steadily eastward-flying VTL, the ground was now reddened by the sun sinking to the horizon behind them. Underneath at this moment was the varicolored patchwork of old farmlands, but the lights of a city glowed on the horizon ahead. Somewhere up ahead there, a Core Tap power station with its massive broadcast antenna crouched over a shaft driven three hundred miles deep into the Earth's hot interior; the heat and pressure at the deep end of that shaft would soon be used to power the heavy generators that would send radiant power from the antenna to the factories and power stations that lighted the city Rafe watched. When that happened, the alpha rhythms of human and animal brains within range of the antenna would be distorted by the power broadcast, and the bodies to which the brains belonged would sleep, whether they needed sleep or not. It was only now, this close to the sunset time at which the power broadcasts from the Core Taps to the food factories were begun, that one of the two other men had finally broken silence.

"All right," said Pao, "you had experience with how you reacted under power broadcast and found it didn't put you as much asleep as it put others. You found out

23

that even with your brain waves in the enforced alpha rhythm you could move about. Even better—maybe you could not only sleepwalk, you could control your sleepwalking to some extent. But do you realize how much more we know about the enforced alpha state now than we did back when the experimental models of the power broadcast units were being tested? We know now that it's not only nervous responses that are affected—it's judgment. In an alpha state induced by the broadcast, you could think you were doing quite well in controlling your actions, but a film taken of you at the time would show you stumbling around, being clumsy, slow, and uncertain in your movements—like someone under narcotics, or drunk if you like. But you wouldn't have realized this. Just like a drunk, you'd have thought how well you were doing."

"That's what the trouble is with people like Lee—and the rest of the world's billions," said Rafe. "They get drunk every night whether they want to or not, and it's starting to pile up on them."

"You're not listening to me," Pao Gallot said.

"No. It's you who're not listening to me," replied Rafe. "Why don't you go a week without using the broadcast station and see what effects show up in the world's populace?"

"Turn them off for a week?" snorted Forebringer. "We couldn't turn them off a single night! We're just barely meeting adequate calorie quotas now. A week with none of the food factories working would put us so far behind we'd have a famine on our hands before we could catch up again!"

"How can you be so sure?" said Rafe.

"Because he's right," said Pao Gallot. "Don't you believe *me?* It's my job to keep the people of the world fed."

"Not that we could go a week anyway," muttered Forebringer. "The first night that word got out the factories weren't producing we'd have full-scale revolution on our hands . . ."

The last word from his lips trailed off oddly. His eyelids wavered and fell. His face slackened. Beside him, Pao was already, suddenly, asleep, round face resting on a roll of neck fat above his cravat.

The interior of the VTL blurred about Rafe. Obviously, they had been inside an area of one of the broadcast stations when its power had just been turned on for the night, rather than having simply flown into a working broadcast area. The effect of any such broadcast fell off sharply after a specified distance, but its edge gradient was still gradual enough that Forebringer would not have dropped asleep in midsentence. Instinctively, Rafe tensed against the impulse smothering him into slumber.

He made himself relax.

Don't fight, he told himself. *Don't fight. Slide with it . . . easy . . . easy . . .*

The "slide" was metaphorical. It was a matter of knowing what could be fought and what could not. He could not stop the power broadcast now filling the atmosphere about him from forcing the electrical activity of his brain into a specific—and soporific—alpha-wave pattern. He could, however, go along with the alpha patterning and find some accommodation with the rest of his body that avoided the soporific effect. It was that same effect that had undoubtedly put the circles under the eyes of the woman Lee and brought a cast of hopelessness to her face. It was the effect that immobilized half of Earth's population during the dark hours—except for the "zombies," those natural immunes, certain yoga-trained individuals, and a very few others who could control their brain-wave patterns consciously. Like Rafe himself?

Slide . . . slide with the push.

Good. Now start to take hold . . . take hold. Now turn . . . push . . . override the flow of the broadcast . . . divert it slightly . . . a little more. . . . Now!

Rafe sat up in the pilot's seat with his eyes open. Except for a strange feeling, something like a wire thrumming inside him, sensed but not heard, he felt perfectly normal. But these would be only his subjective reactions.

He brought his left wrist around in front of his eyes and focused on the dial of his watch. It looked as always —except that the second hand seemed to be whirling about the circular face at four or five times its normal speed, while the longer minute hand crept perceptibly forward in matching time.

Reflexes, he thought, and almost laughed. *From someone with the world's fastest to a man with some of the slowest.*

The humorous reaction threatened to upset his accommodation with the broadcast pattern. For a moment the aircraft cabin blurred around him again, and the heavy hand of drowsiness was laid upon him like the paw of a bear, pulling him down. He leaned back and rode it out.

Easy . . . easy. The watch was only one aspect of the universe. Time was relative. The broadcast pattern was only another aspect. Space distorted still remained space. Time distorted remained time. In the perception was all . . . all. No aspect of space or time or universe had any hold on him. They were all relative, all peripheral to his being. *I am the center of my universe . . .*

He was back, once more in control of himself. He looked again at the watch.

Slow down, he told the second hand. *Slow . . .*

For a little while it continued to whirl as if ignoring him. Then, gradually, it seemed to slow while he kept his gaze steady on it. Slower . . . slower . . . Still, not as slow as normal, but good enough.

He turned his attention back to the VTL.

They were already over the lighted city, and the aircraft had been caught up by ground control into what would have been the traffic pattern over the local landing field if there had been any other traffic in the air to make up a pattern. One conventional swing about the field and then the ground equipment would try to bring it in—and this VTL was not equipped to respond to the proper automatic signals from below.

Rafe flicked the switch excusing the aircraft from ground control and signaling the automatic equipment below that he was coming in on manual.

He brought the craft down lightly just beyond the main terminal building. Outside, everything was brightly lit, but there was nothing moving. Working against a heavy weight of inertia that invited him to give up all this effort, he got to his feet, went back past his two slumbering passengers, and stepped down onto the brilliantly lit concrete.

The night breeze blew coolly on his face, but the refreshment it brought him was only to the surface of his skin. Even the feel of the moving air was somehow remote and lonely.

He turned and plodded, rather than walked, in through the empty terminal building, past deserted restaurants and magazine booths and airline counters, and across a vast, clean stretch of imitation yellow-marble flooring. The sound of the heels of his high boots clacked loudly, echoing and re-echoing, back and forth in the emptiness between the floor and the high, concrete-ribbed ceiling of the building.

He walked through a wide air-curtain door, feeling the draft of air remotely on his face, like the breeze outside. To his left were ranked dark shadows—the rental car stand. He ignored it, looking around. To his right and stretching away under bright flood lamps was a parking lot full of private vehicles. He turned and plodded toward them, and when he arrived at the first row, began methodically going down their rank, trying door handles to find one that was unlocked.

He found a door that opened on the fourteenth or fifteenth two-wheeler he tried. But it was not until he had worked his way halfway down the second rank of parked vehicles that he found one not only with open doors, but with the motor lock-switch open.

He climbed into the seat behind its control stick and tried the instruments. They showed the vehicle ready to roll except for two half-discharged cells. He wheeled it out of the parking lot and stopped at the service station at the edge of the field to smash a door lock with a jack handle and replace the two half-depleted cells with new ones. Then he drove on out to the highway and checked the car's autolocator.

The small dashboard map that lit up on the control-panel screen showed a green dot at an airfield just outside of El Dorado, Kansas. He had swung south in flying east from Oregon.

He cut back to the northwest now to pick up a freeway with an unlimited-speed strip. There were no traffic police during the night hours any more, and he might have taken any roadway he wanted—but only unlimited strips were engineered for uncontrolled vehicles with speeds up to three hundred miles an hour, though this three- or four-year-old jalopy he had stolen seemed unlikely to be in tune to do more than two hundred.

He joined the freeway at Newton and drove northeast at top speed through Emporia, past sleeping Kansas City and silent Independence, then swung north to St. Joseph and up into Iowa, turned east at Des Moines, and rolled into the brightly lit, utterly quiet suburb of Des Moines that was the college town of Grinnell, as the local time clock on his car's instrument panel showed twenty-eight minutes past eleven.

Approximately seven more hours of dark and broadcast power. A little more than seven hours before Forebringer would be able to get out a world-wide police bulletin on him.

Warning lights blinked at him unexpectedly across the street ahead. He jerked the control stick back, throwing the motor sharply into retrograde. The tires squealed deafeningly in the silence, but he lost speed safely.

Now, right up to the lights, he could see that there had been excavation in the street—some sort of work that had torn up the pavement. A narrow way seemed open next to the left curb where there was a gap in the line of flashers. He steered for it.

As he entered the opening in the flasher line, he had a second in which to notice that the street light just beyond the torn-up area was out, so that the space beyond the warning lights was a pool of blackness. Then the nose of the car dropped, and the front wheel lurched down into something soft and stuck. The vehicle spun sideways and the motor died. He reached for his waistband, but the pill-gun was gone. It must have worked loose and dropped out earlier. Outside the windshield a shadow moved.

It had barely stopped moving when he was out of the door at his left, moving instinctively. He had a momentary, kaleidoscopic image of a black figure, arm upraised against the lighter dark of the sky; then as the arm came down, he had dived past and collided with another figure, a human body. Fury woke in him.

For a moment the two of them tumbled together in the sand, or dirt, or whatever it was. Then Rafe got knee and fist home to soft parts of the body and rolled to one side, looking upward. Once more, the first figure—and now he recognized that it carried a club in its upraised hand—loomed above him.

He rolled again. The club came down harmlessly to earth. He was on his feet before the club-wielder had begun to recover balance. Slowly, ponderously, like a shape in a dream, it was coming erect again, lifting its arm. Rafe struck out savagely at the point between head and shoulders, this time with the edge of his hand, and felt the impact of his blow against the neck of the figure. It sagged backward, fell, and lay in the light of the single head lamp of the stalled car, a heavy man in his early forties, a knife at his belt and the club fallen from his grasp, trying to breathe with both hands at his throat.

"You're lucky I couldn't see better," Rafe told him bitterly. "I'd have broken your neck."

He became aware suddenly that the thrumming feeling inside him had gone. But now that he thought of it, it began to be noticeable again. It grew once more inside him, an ugly, unnatural feeling of his body being used without his consent. He looked again at the man choking on the ground.

"Yes, indeed," he said softly to himself, "there are zombies."

He walked around, got back into the car, and directed the headlight over on the first man he had hit. That man lay without struggling, unconscious.

Rafe turned his attention to the car itself. By sweeping the headlight around he could see that he was in a shallow, sandy excavation with firm pavement just a few feet to his right. The zombies had evidently moved the warning lights to leave unguarded the hole in the road they were meant to protect.

Rafe triggered the car's motor back to life and tried rocking it, cautiously. The wheels spun, digging into the sand, but after a few seconds, he built up enough momentum to lurch the front wheel onto the solid pavement.

He switched all power to that front wheel and pushed the stick forward. With a jerk and a surge, the car pulled itself up out of the hole.

He wheeled on down the road, checking his memory for the address he wanted—5514 Busher Drive. He checked a map of Grinnell's streets on the control-panel autolocator. He was not far from it. A few seconds later he swung into a curving street that bent off to the right of the one on which he was traveling. BUSHER DRIVE said the street sign, and he drove slowly along it, looking for house numbers that could be read in the light of his head lamp.

On either side the houses were old and large. Houses like this had not been built for nearly fifty years. They sat back from the street, either fenced or hedged from the eyes of anyone passing. He searched several gates and entrances with his head lamp before he located the number 5504. Fifty-five fourteen should be close then . . .

It was the house just beyond. It had a six-foot woven

wire fence with a top bar and massed greenery thick within it. Both its walk and driveway entrances were gated and chained, but the number 5514 gleamed in some reflective substance from a post upholding one of the driveway gates.

Rafe stopped the car and got out. He tried the driveway gates, but the chain chinked and held. He went down along the wall to the walk gate and found it as heavily secured by another chain. He looked up at the top of the wire fence, but projecting above the top bar were the sharp ends of cut wire. For a moment he thought of charging the driveway gate with the car.

But there was no space for him to get up speed, and both gates and chain looked strong enough to stop him. He looked up and down the sidewalk below the fence. A large boulevard elm had heavy branches projecting in over the fence above the grounds of 5514.

The elm was too big to get his arms around, and its lowest branches had been trimmed off to perhaps fifteen feet above the ground. He unbuckled the belt around his waist, pulled it out, and looped one end through the buckle around his left wrist. Throwing the tongue of the belt around the tree, he caught it in his other hand, and slowly, against the difficulties of the rough, spongy bark and the clumsiness of his slowed-down reflexes, he began to inchworm his way up the branchless lower trunk.

After a few minutes, he came within grasping distance of the lowest branch, and hung onto it, gratefully, getting his breath back. After a few seconds, he pulled himself up until he was seated on the branch, and replaced the belt in its trouser loops.

The branch he was on was not one of those which extended out over the fence, above the grounds of 5514. He had to climb another four feet to find one that did. He straddled this limb and began inching his way out along its length.

For the first dozen feet or so, it bore him firmly. But then as the branch narrowed, it began to bend downward under his weight. This was all to the good—this was what he had counted on, since the point where branch met tree trunk was twenty feet off the ground and he had hoped to get a good deal closer to the lawn inside the fence before jumping.

But then as the branch creaked behind him and began

to dip dangerously toward the breaking point, he paused and looked below. He was a good fifteen feet inside the fence and its tall hedge, and the ground was barely ten feet below him. There was nothing in sight to alarm him. So why had he hesitated?

Then he heard it again—and recognized it as the sound that had triggered his inner alarm without his consciously identifying it. It was a low-pitched, growling whine.

His eyes searched for the maker of the sound below him in the darkness—and this time he found it.

It was a wolf, a male timber wolf, fully adult, weighing perhaps a hundred and forty pounds. It stood just below him on the lawn, tail half curved and motionless behind it, the jaws a little open, broad brow and eyes that were catching and reflecting the distant glint of the street light. The wolf gazed steadily up at him. There was a glint as of something metal above its brow, between the upheld, pointed ears.

The whining growl broke off. It became all whine and shaped itself into chewed, barely recognizable words.

"I am Lucas," the wolf said. "And I have been told to kill."

4

Instinctively, Rafe tried to back up. But the branch dipped under him at the movement, and without visibly setting himself for the effort, the wolf shot into the air toward him. Rafe jerked his dangling feet up level with the branch, and white teeth clicked shut only inches below them as the branch lifted again. Rafe clung to it, not moving.

Slowed by the broadcast power as he was, he had no intention of taking his chances on the ground with a beast like the one below. There had to be other ways of handling this situation than facing a timber wolf with his bare hands.

Lucas was still singing below him in a wavering combination of growl and whine. Feet hooked on the branch now, Rafe leaned forward a little—the branch trembled beneath him—and spoke to the wolf.

"Lucas," he said. "I'm here to see someone you know. Gabrielle. Can Gabrielle hear me if I talk to you?"

The growling whine broke off for a moment, then picked up again.

"Gabrielle?" said Rafe, raising his voice slightly. "This is Rafe Harald. I talked to you on the phone yesterday—or maybe it was the day before yesterday, now—from the Moon, about Ab. I've gone to a lot of trouble to get here, but Lucas has me trapped on a branch above your front lawn and I can't go backward or forward."

He waited. There was no response but the steady, throaty warning of the wolf.

"Gabrielle," said Rafe loudly. "If you're Ab's sister, you know about his work. So do I. That ought to prove I'm no zombie. I know that Ab probably found some way of shielding people against the broadcast influence—or some way of counteracting it. The fact that Lucas here is moving around when the power's on, in the middle of the night, shows Ab did something like that. If he did, that means that you can probably move around when the power's on, too. You ought to be able to come out here and keep Lucas off me long enough for me to prove who I am. Gabrielle, can you hear me?"

Still no answer but the sound of the wolf. Rafe looked down.

"All right, Lucas," he said. "I want to talk to Gabrielle. *Gabrielle*. Where's Gabrielle?"

The whine broke into a word.

"No," said Lucas.

"You're not the one to judge," said Rafe. "Gabrielle will decide. Gabrielle wouldn't want you to hurt me. I can't seem to call her, but you can, I know. Call Gabrielle."

"No," said Lucas.

"Why not? Did Gabrielle tell you never to call her?"

"No." The wolf licked his jaws and whined, his eyes bright and steady on Rafe.

"Then call her. Gabrielle would want you to call her when I come."

"No. You're lying to me," said Lucas. "Gabrielle would have told me if I was to call her."

"She didn't know I was coming this soon," said Rafe. "Look, you go get her. I'll stay right here."

"No. But you stay."

"Lucas—" Rafe shifted the grip of his aching fingers on the branch. His balance on it with his feet up was precarious, sustained only by muscle power. Soon, before he lost his grip entirely, he would have to let himself drop and take his chances with Lucas if he could not talk the wolf into contacting Gabrielle. "Lucas, listen. Ab's gone, isn't he?"

Whine and growl from below. No answer.

"That's right. Ab's gone," said Rafe. "And someone's keeping him prisoner somewhere—" Rafe wondered for a second, fleetingly, how much of this Lucas could understand. "Any moment now, the same people who took Ab may come to take Gabrielle—"

The whine and growl in Lucas's throat rose to pure growl, to a snarl like thunder on the horizon.

"Unless I can get to Gabrielle and help her, first," said Rafe. "They'll take Gabrielle away from you unless you call her for me, right now. Think, Lucas. It's up to you.

You want to do what's right. You want to call Gabrielle
and save her. Call Gabrielle, or they'll come and take
her away . . ."

Rafe let his words trail off. Lucas was slowly backing
up along the ground, moving backward from below the
branch.

"Good, Lucas," said Rafe. "Very good. Call Gabrielle."

Rumbling in his throat, brilliant-eyed with reflected
street light, shoulders hunched and tail low, Lucas continued to back away. Suddenly, with an abrupt howl, he
turned and raced off into the darkness. For a long second
there was silence, and Rafe hastily tried to release his
cramped fingers from around the branch so that he could
at least retreat to the tree before Lucas came back. Then
the deafening clangor of an alarm bell erupted into life,
and the exterior of a two-story, half-timbered house burst
into appearance a hundred feet from him as floodlights
went on all around it.

Gratefully, Rafe let go of his branch and dropped. He
hardly felt his landing on the turf and rolled over on his
back, stretching his aching arms and numb fingers. He
started to lift his head—

And froze. The deep, throaty rumbling of a growl was
just beside him. He turned his head slowly, and looked
into Lucas's face, inches from his own. The wolf was
crouched beside him, his partly open jaws almost touching Rafe's throat.

"I won't move," whispered Rafe. "Easy, Lucas. Easy . . ."

The rumbling growl went on. Wolf breath blew into
Rafe's nostrils, and saliva dripped from the open jaws
onto Rafe's neck. He felt its coolness through the cloth
of his cravat.

"I won't move," Rafe said. "Don't worry, Lucas. I
won't move."

They stayed together without change for several more
minutes. Then, abruptly, the clanging alarm bell shut off
in mid-ring, but Rafe's ears continued to echo the sound
of it. There was what seemed like a long time of waiting
before Lucas's growl broke abruptly into a whine again,
and his head shifted slightly to look beyond and behind the
top of Rafe's head.

"Gabrielle?" said Rafe. He was careful to continue to lie
still. "Are you there? I'm Rafe Harald, from the Far-Star

Project on the Moon. I talked to you on the phone about Ab's being gone, yesterday or the day before."

The whisper of something like a little breeze approached the top of his head. Lucas's jaws were still at his throat, and Rafe did not dare turn his head to see.

"Gabrielle?" he said.

"What's your middle name?" The feminine voice was young, but unyielding.

"Arnoul," said Rafe. "Rafael Arnoul Harald. When I called you the other day, I reminded you that Ab and I used to drink beer in a little three-two joint just off campus. But I didn't tell you its name. It was the Blue Jug. You'd just gotten into high school then. Ab was eight years older than I was—and looked younger. Your mother and dad had just died two or three years before. Ask me anything else you want to know."

"You can get up," her voice said, "in a minute. Lucas will bring you to me in the house. If you've got any weapons, leave them outside."

"I haven't," he said.

There was again that strange whisper like a breeze on the grass, going away from him. He looked at Lucas. After a moment, the wolf rose, backed off slightly, and sat down, now making no sound at all.

Rafe got slowly to his feet. Lucas rose again and moved off. Rafe turned and began to walk toward the brilliantly lit house. A glance back over his shoulder showed Lucas following, head low.

They reached the front of the house.

"Which way, Lucas?" asked Rafe. "The front steps?"

"Yes," said Lucas.

They went toward the front steps and up them. The front door was not only unlocked but ajar. Rafe stepped in through it, and Lucas pushed through at his heels. Rafe turned to close the door and saw Lucas watching him.

"That's right, isn't it?" Rafe said. "Should I close the door?"

"I'll do it," said Lucas.

He rose on his legs, putting his front paws against the door and pushing it closed with his weight. The latch clicked. There was a heavy metal bolt above the doorknob. Lucas took the fingerknob of the bolt in his teeth and pulled it closed. Then he dropped back onto four legs, once more facing Rafe.

"Now where, Lucas?"

"Back." The wolf herded him down a central passageway to a door which let them into a room that seemed half a physical laboratory, half an electrical repair shop. At the far end of the room was a high bench or worktable with a solid front. Visible behind the bench from the waist up, facing him, was a brown-haired, long-boned, and startlingly pretty young woman who at first glance seemed to show no resemblance to the thirteen- or fourteen-year-old girl Rafe barely remembered from his university days. Only the rather wide mouth, which he remembered as capable of flashing sudden, all-encompassing smiles, was familiar. It was not smiling now.

Lucas whined.

"That's all right, Lucas," she said. "You don't have to come in. Wait just outside the door—but leave the door open."

With something close to a single wag of his tail Lucas turned and went back through the doorway he and Rafe had just entered. He lay down just outside.

"He's not afraid of anything in here, Mr. Harald—if that's really who you are," Gabrielle said. "So don't think he isn't guarding you this minute. It's just that something about this place makes him unhappy."

"It's where Ab did the work on him, I suppose?" said Rafe.

She shot a suddenly suspicious glance at him.

"Work?" she said. "What work?"

"There's something on his skull between the ears," answered Rafe. "I can't see it here in the light, but I caught a glint from it, outside. And he does talk. That would be Ab's sort of work, tying in somehow to the electrical responses of the brain in certain situations and using that tie-in to trigger sets of vocal responses. Something like that?"

She gazed at him for a long moment.

"You're doing a lot of guessing, aren't you?" Her voice was dry.

"Am I?" Rafe answered. "But there's the evidence—the talking and whatever there is on his skull. Although, come to think of it, I don't suppose most people know enough about a timber wolf's skull to recognize a change in its shape."

"Most people," she said, and her voice was warmer

now, "don't know enough to know a timber wolf from a dog."

"They do if they've got dogs of their own along when they get close to the wolf," said Rafe. "Haven't any of your neighbors complained?"

"None of the neighbors close around here have dogs," she said. "Besides, I keep Lucas indoors during the day and only let him out at night. But I know what you mean. Any of the dogs around here that've seen Lucas, or smelled him, seem scared silly."

The initial suspicion was fading from her voice.

"With reason," said Rafe.

"Probably." She looked at him. "You certainly sound like Rafe the way I remember him. It was only once I saw you—when you dropped by the house to pick up Ab —and that was all."

"There were also the graduation ceremonies when Ab got his doctorate," said Rafe.

Gabrielle sighed suddenly like someone putting down a loaded weapon that was no longer needed.

"All right," she said, "You're Rafe."

"Thanks," said Rafe. "Can I call you Gaby?"

"I never liked the name—" Suddenly she laughed. "But all right. Why not? Somehow, the way you say it, I don't mind." Her face sobered. "How did you get here so fast? And traveling at night? How did you know you could move around when the broadcast was on?"

He laughed, a little shakily because of the exhaustion possessing him.

"Is there some place we can go and sit down?" he said. "Then I'll tell you anything you want to know. I've been on the run since I left the Moon."

"Of course," she said.

She came around the end of the bench with the same small sound of a breeze blowing he had heard before— and she was traveling in an upright cylinder that fitted her to the waist and slid along on innumerable tiny jets of air.

"That's right," she said, meeting his eyes, "I've been paralyzed from the waist down for three years. But Ab was helping me get over it. I was one of the first night's accidents."

"First night's accidents?" He followed her as she glided ahead of him, leading the way out into the central pas-

sageway and from there through another door into what
was obviously a living room—a green-wallpapered room
with heavy couches and armchairs. Lucas followed them
in and curled up beside one of the chairs as she rode her
vehicle to the very edge of the chair, then tilted its cylinder backward, and slid out into the chair. Relieved of her
weight, the cylinder returned to upright position again,
and the two rested like sentinels on either side of her—
the whispering vehicle and the wolf.

Rafe dropped into a chair opposite her. The thrumming
inside him was wearing him down, like a nagging pain. He
had to fight consciously against the urge to close his eyes
and give in to the soporific effect.

"Have you got any stimulants?" he asked.

She looked at him sharply.

"Dexedrine," she said. "But it won't help you against
the broadcast."

He grimaced, running a hand over his neck as if to
clamp down on the top end of the thrumming feeling
within him.

"Let me try some, anyway."

She turned to the wolf.

"Lucas," she said. "In the doughnut-to-fennel drawer
of the lab. Package egg/potato."

Lucas rose and went out.

"He's an amazing animal," said Rafe, looking after him.
"The talking's complicated enough. How'd you get him
to memorize codes?"

"It's an easy code for him," she said. "We've got an
alphabet of kitchen odors—A for apple, B for bread, and
E for egg and P for potato, in this case. I file things al-
phabetically and rub each filed item with one to three of
the coded substances. His nose does the rest."

Lucas came back in with a heavy brown bottle in his
jaws.

"Take it to Rafe," she said. Lucas brought the bottle and
dropped it on Rafe's knees. He opened it and took out a
couple of heart-shaped orange pills, looking at them dis-
tastefully. One of them, after a second, he put back in
the bottle.

"Come to think of it, you'll want some water—"

"No need." He interrupted her, and hastily gulped down
the single pill he held.

"One's not enough to do you any good, anyway," she said.

"Don't be too sure—" he broke off, interrupting himself. "How long until daylight?"

"This time of year?" she said. "Maybe four hours, now."

"And the broadcast goes off at daylight?"

"Soon after that." She looked at him curiously. "Why?"

"Because by daylight, you and I are going to have to be far away from here. Never mind that now, though," he said. "You were telling me you were one of the first night's accidents? What first night?"

"Didn't you read about it even up on the Moon?" she said. "The first night they turned on the power broadcasts, everybody had been warned to be safely tucked away at home before sunset when the power would go on. I was one of the ones who shaved my time too thin getting home. I was driving back to the house here when the broadcast came on. When I woke up next morning, I was still pinned in the wreck of the car I'd crashed twelve hours before. They got me out a couple of hours later, and they patched me up. But my legs didn't work."

"Nerve damage?" he said.

"Nothing physiological they could find," she answered. "They told Ab it had to be psychological. He didn't believe them, bless him!" She blinked rapidly a couple of times. "His theory was that while I was unconscious the continuous power broadcast had conditioned my normal brain-wave pattern—held it distorted long enough so that it couldn't snap back to normal again."

"Well," said Rafe. "That was his field—brain-wave patterns."

"Yes," she said fiercely, "and no one understood what he'd done in it—no one!"

The thrumming inside Rafe was getting worse instead of better. He folded his arms and pressed back hard against his middle.

"Something the matter?" said Gaby quickly. "You're shaking!"

He managed a small grin.

"I've got a hunch taking that dexedrine was a mistake," he said.

"Then why on earth did you take it?"

The thrumming mounted within him. He felt as if he were shaking apart.

"Never can tell how drugs will work with me," he said between teeth that were starting to chatter in spite of everything he could do. "Never could take stimulants—on the other hand, had to load me with sleeping pills when they wanted me to sleep. Thought—maybe with the broadcast, things could be reversed—worth trying, anyhow . . ."

The chattering of his teeth and the thrumming inside him were becoming too strong to permit him the luxury of spending effort on talking.

"There's got to be something that'll help you!"

"Sedative. Depressant. Any liquor handy—"

"Lucas! Dining room. Scotch—"

But Lucas was already on his feet, tense and motionless, head pointed toward the front of the house. Slowly his head moved and a barely heard rumble of a growl sounded in him.

"What is it, Lucas?" said Gaby. "What—"

"Four," said Lucas, who was now slowly turning around in a full circle. "One, front door. One, driveway gate. Two at back of house."

"Four? Four what? Zombies?"

Rafe forced his head up, struggling to ignore the thrumming and the teeth-chattering for long enough to understand what was going on—and suddenly the room was full of shadows.

Four shadows, like black paper cutouts of men with clubs in their hands, were converging on him. He flung himself forward out of the chair, lunging stiff-armed at the midsection of the closest shadow, to break clear of the ring of them before they could close in on him. His fist sank home. Something struck heavily but glancingly against his shoulder. He heard the mounting snarl of Lucas, and the wolf had joined him in the fight. Rafe kicked devastatingly at another of the shadow figures, and it went down in front of him. Suddenly he was struck again, this time heavily on the side of the head.

He stumbled, falling, into a blur of darkness.

5

He woke again to find Gaby out of her vehicle, seated on the carpet beside him, and supporting his head while she held a small glass at his lips. He drank—and choked. It was undiluted Scotch whisky. He shook his head and turned his lips away from the glass.

"No need, now—" he had to stop to cough. "I'm all right."

And, in fact, he was. Even as he said the words, he realized that the thrumming and the pressure of the soporific effect was gone from him, as it had been momentarily after his earlier encounter with the zombies on the street under repair. He lifted his head and looked around. There was no sign of shadow figures in the room, and Lucas sat with his fur unruffled.

"Where'd they go?" Rafe asked Gaby. "What were they?"

"I don't know." She looked at him strangely, sitting back with the glass of Scotch still in her hand. "I didn't see anything."

"Didn't see anything?" He stared at her. "Four black shadows like men with clubs?"

"Is that what they were?" She shook her head. "No, I didn't see them. But Lucas was fighting them too; so they were here, all right."

"And they were real, all right," said Rafe. He felt the side of his head where something had struck him. It was tender and swelling under the scalp.

"Two, I killed," said Lucas. "You killed the others."

"Killed?" Rafe looked at the wolf. "What were they, Lucas?"

"Men," said the wolf. "Men with no smell. What's left is outside."

"Outside?" Rafe scrambled to his feet. "That reminds me. We've got to get out of here, Gaby. We can talk on the way, but we've got to get going. I practically hijacked a shuttle, and I did kidnap Pao Gallot and Bill Fore-bringer to get here. As soon as it's day, the police'll be looking for me. You've got to come with me. There're too many questions and not enough time to answer them here."

Gaby reached back with one hand for her vehicle, which stood behind her, and tipped the cylinder down. She turned and slid her legs back into it, then pushed with one arm against the rug. As if counterweighed, the cylinder swung back upright with her in it.

"All right," she said. "We'll go—all three of us. Just give me five minutes to pack a few things."

"Do you have to—all right, yes," said Rafe. The thrumming was just beginning to make itself felt inside him again, and some nervous element inside him was rubbed raw by it. He looked about, picked up the glass of Scotch Gaby had been offering him earlier. He drank it down.

"I thought you said you didn't want it?" she asked on her way out of the room.

"We'll find out—" he began to answer, but she was already gone. He looked for the wolf and found Lucas sitting on the rug. Their eyes met.

"So," said Rafe. "Men without smells."

"Yes," said Lucas.

A slight shiver ran down Rafe's spine. There was something terrible, with a terribleness transcending a sick and near-starving world, in two-dimensional shadows that could enter a brightly lit room like this to try and kill. Shadows that vanished after they were fought off.

"But you said what's left is outside?" Rafe asked the wolf.

"All four men. Dead," said Lucas.

"You mean"—Rafe thought for a second—"what came into the room here was part of the four men you smelled—"

"Heard."

"Heard outside the house? Who could that be?"

Lucas merely stared back at him.

"What's that mean when you don't answer?" Rafe asked. "You mean you don't know?"

"I don't know," said Lucas.

"But you say the men and the shadows were the same. How do you know that?"

"I don't know," said Lucas. "But the same. I know. But I don't know."

"You mean you know how they could be the same, but you don't know how to tell me?" Rafe asked.

"No. I don't know how, but they were the same. I know that. Man-shadow, shadow-man—all the same. To me, all one. To you, don't see how. To Gabrielle, nothing there."

Rafe frowned thoughtfully.

"She really didn't see them . . ." he said, half to himself.

"Didn't see, feel. They didn't see, feel her. No touch between them."

"How do you know?" Rafe said. "How do you know all this?"

"I . . . see," said Lucas. "You don't see. No more. That's all of talk. It's no use."

The wolf dropped down into lying position and began to lick at his forepaw. Rafe took a step closer. Slicked down by the wet tongue, the hair of the foreleg revealed a cut and a swelling on the leg. Rafe dropped on one knee and reached out a hand to examine the leg.

Lucas growled. Rafe drew back his hand.

"No," the wolf said.

"I just wanted to have a look at it, Lucas," Rafe said. "Maybe I can help."

"No," said Lucas.

Rafe got back on his feet.

A couple of minutes later Gaby came into the room, carrying a small black overnight bag.

"Ready," she said. "We'll go out the kitchen door to the garage. The car's there."

Rafe and Lucas followed her. They went through the house to the kitchen, and through a door in its far wall. Gaby opened the door and switched on the light beyond. Rafe got a glimpse of the interior of a three-car garage and both a large and small two-wheeler.

"We'd better take the big car," she said, and looked at Rafe. "You'll drive?"

"I'll drive," he said.

They got into the larger two-wheeler, and Rafe took it out of the garage carefully. It was a good, powerful vehicle, and in tune. Good for perhaps two hundred and fifty, flat out.

He backed it down the driveway toward the locked gates closing the driveway and stopped. Gaby handed him a key.

"Right," he said. He got out and went back to unlock the chain securing the gates. As the lock opened and the chain fell apart, he saw a dark figure crumpled on the lawn about twenty feet away. He finished pushing the gates open, then went over to bend above the figure.

It was the body of a man. The motionless, staring eyes and the contorted face, seen in the reflected glare of the floodlights on the house, were enough to see—without testing further for evidence—that the man was dead. There was no wound upon him, but both hands were balled into fists, protectively, at his throat; and the arms were so tightly cramped that they resisted when Rafe tried to pull the fists away. A whine behind Rafe made him start.

Lucas pushed past Rafe and sniffed at the dead man.

"One of yours, was he, Lucas?" said Rafe, looking at those clenched hands. The little shiver he had felt earlier returned to his spine. "But what sort of sympathetic magic made him die out here, without a mark on him?"

Lucas made no answer.

Rafe turned abruptly.

"Back to the car," he said, turning on his heel. "We've got to get out of here."

But when he went around the car and slid once more behind the control stick, he glanced back and saw Lucas still standing over the dead man.

"Lucas!" he called.

The wolf did not respond. Instead, he sat down suddenly and lifted his muzzle to the sky. He howled—a long, eerie, quavering howl.

"What's wrong with him? Gaby," said Rafe, "we've got to get out of here. Call him back to the car."

"Lucas!" Gaby called. *"Lucas!"*

But Lucas continued to howl, ignoring even her.

"Damn!" said Gaby. She twisted about in the seat. They had put her cylindrical vehicle across the curve of the back lounge seat of the car. "Help me, Rafe. I'll have to go after him."

Rafe reached back to help her get the awkwardly large cylinder up where she could slide into it.

"What's the matter?" he asked. "Won't he come when you call?"

She flashed him a glance that was almost angry.

"You don't understand!" she said. "He's a wolf, not a dog. Ab left him that way."

"What's the difference?" Rafe asked.

"He's a person—that's the difference!" She was into her vehicle now and a second later was upright, gliding over the grass. She came up to where Lucas still howled, his wild cry splitting the otherwise silent night, nose pointed at the sky. She took hold of what was evidently a collar hidden in the rough, long fur of his neck and pulled hard, using the drive of her vehicle to reinforce her efforts.

"*Lucas!*" she said.

The wolf allowed himself to be dragged to all four feet. His howling ceased. She turned and drove back to the car. He followed behind her, head and tail held low.

Gaby got back into the car and Rafe got her vehicle once more onto the rear lounge seat. Then she reached out, took hold of Lucas's collar, and pulled him into the front seat of the car with them.

"Now we can go," she said.

Rafe backed out into the street, turned, and drove off. The thrumming was back inside him now, but so was the Scotch. The liquor was like a pad between a raw spot and something savagely chafing. The relief, as much as the alcohol, made him a little lightheaded. He looked across at the furry mask of Lucas.

"Gaby says you're a person," he told the wolf.

The wild face looked back at him.

"I am Lucas," said Lucas.

Rafe nodded slowly, turning back to his driving and his watch on the street ahead.

"Where are we going?" asked Gaby. "I haven't even asked."

"As far away as we can get by sunrise," said Rafe soberly. "But first—there's a spot I want to look at again . . ." He told her about the two zombies and the ambush by the spot where the street was under repair.

"But why?"

"Who were they waiting for?" Rafe asked. "Me? But how could they know I was coming? And who else would be moving around during the broadcast? Or do they have gang wars at night, these zombies?"

"In Grinnell?" Gaby said. "Don't be ridiculous. Don't you know the zombies—I mean, all people with resistance, natural or trained, to the broadcasts—are less than two in every million of population? The whole Des Moines metropolitan area can't have more than half a dozen."

"In that case," said Rafe, "I've met them all tonight."

"But—" She broke off. For a moment she was silent. Then she went on in a subdued voice. "It still doesn't make sense. What do you know about zombies?"

"Not enough," said Rafe grimly. "Wait—" His headlight had once more picked up the site of the road repair. It seemed deserted, but he drove up to it cautiously and swept the headlight all around, carefully, before getting out of the car.

There was nothing to be seen, only the warning blinkers falsely set up to direct a driver into the hole in the road, and the scoured-up sand in the bottom of the hole itself. Rafe stepped down into the hole and looked around, but discovered nothing that might give any clue to the identity of the two who had ambushed and attacked him.

Lucas shoved past him, nose to the sandy bottom of the hole. He cast about, snorted some dust from his nostrils, and then moved away up the side of the hole next to the curb.

"This way," Lucas said.

Rafe followed Lucas, and the wolf followed his nose along the ground. They crossed the grassy boulevard, a corner of a front lawn, and went down a narrow midblock alley until Lucas abruptly turned in behind a tall, untrimmed hedge of Japanese barberry.

Rafe followed. There, in the deep shadow of the bushes, was a short-bodied but heavy-engined sport two-wheeler, obviously built for speed. Rafe opened the closest door.

Inside, the body of a man lay dumped on his back on the narrow lounge seat, and his skin was already cold to the touch. It was the man Rafe had hit in the neck. Slumped over the control stick was another man, unconscious.

Rafe felt through the pockets of both men, but outside of a couple of wallets with money, they carried nothing. The control-panel compartment and trunk compartment also were empty except for a road map of the Grinnell area. Rafe felt around under the front seats and came out with a fuel-cell receipt from a service station with the address Crazian's Corner, Nipigon, Ontario, Canada.

He tucked it in his pocket and went out around the back of the car to look at the license. Sure enough, it was an Ontario license.

He went back to Gaby and their own car. This time, Lucas leaped into the rear lounge seat and curled up. Rafe took the control stick and drove them back the way he had come in, and out onto the freeway. He turned north.

"You found something back there, then," said Gaby, as the car swung at last onto the unlimited-speed strip and he set it on autopilot.

He told her.

"All the way from Canada, down here?" she said. "I don't see the sense of it."

"Or the sense of four other men dead back at your house?" said Rafe. "There wasn't any reason for either setup except for you—to keep me from getting to you from talking to you once I did reach you. And not even you knew I was coming down from the Moon today. Who could know enough to have zombies waiting for me?"

She did not answer immediately. He glanced from the highway ahead over to her. She sat with her shoulders hunched, her arms held tight to her as if she were shivering, suddenly, in an unexpected breath of chill wind.

"The Old Man, maybe," she said.

"The Old Man?" He stared at her. "You mean whoever it is that's supposed to have power over all the zombies. What's his name—Thebom Shankar?"

"Thebom Shankar, the Old Man, Shaitan," she said, still huddled up as if against the cold. "Whatever you want to call him. He's supposed to be a thousand years old and be able to make ghosts and devils fight for him—like whatever it was you and Lucas fought at the house tonight."

For a third time—and he was not used to such feelings; a surge of anger rose suddenly inside him at the reaction—Rafe felt the chill touch on his spine.

"What're you talking about?" he said harshly. "There can't be any such man!"

"But there is," she said. "Ab talked to him on the phone, the day before Ab disappeared."

6

For a long minute nothing was said. The car hummed its way northward along the unlimited-speed strip through dark farmland where all ordinary creatures, human and animal, slept in their druggedlike slumber.

"Let's get this straight," said Rafe at last. "We're talking about the same man, aren't we? The one who's supposed to have some kind of occult power over anyone who can resist the broadcast enough to move around at night?"

"Yes," said Gaby. "The Old Man of the Mountain."

"The Old Man of the Mountain," said Rafe roughly, "was the head of the so-called Assassins, the leader of the Isma'ih sect of Shi'ite Muslims in 1090, who first seized and held the mountain castle of Alamut for his headquarters. And his name was Hasan ibn al-Sabbah, not Thebom Shankar or anything like that."

"I know," she said, still huddled up. "I looked him up in the history books after Ab talked to him."

"What did Ab talk to him about?"

"I don't know." She shook her head. "I came into the lab and Ab was talking on the phone there. I couldn't see the screen, and he broke the connection right away. I said, 'Who was that?' I was just kidding. I don't know what made me say it. 'The Old Man himself?' And Ab's face went white . . . so white . . ."

Her voice trailed off.

"What did he say when you said that?" demanded Rafe.

"He said . . . 'yes,' " she answered. "As if he had to tell me the truth whether he wanted to or not. But when I tried to talk to him some more about it, he wouldn't say a word. That night, he put that bolt lock on the front door and locked himself up for nearly four hours in the lab with Lucas."

"With Lucas?" Rafe looked back at the wolf.

"Lucas," he said. "What happened that night just before Ab left that Gaby's talking about? What did Ab do when you were in the lab with him?"

Lucas looked back at him without answering.

"Rafe, it's no use your asking," Gaby said. "Do you think I haven't asked Lucas? And if he won't tell me, he certainly won't tell you."

"I have to guard," said Lucas unexpectedly. He yawned, his long, wicked-looking carnassials glinting yellowly in the little light from the instrument panel. "Ab and Gabrielle. And I can kill."

He closed his jaws again and sat, as quietly inoffensive-looking as any bushy-furred domestic dog.

"Lucas," said Rafe. "Where's Ab now? Do you know?"

"No," said the wolf. "But we'll find him."

Rafe turned back to Gaby.

"I hope so," he said.

"That's what you came down from the Moon for, isn't it?" Gaby asked. "To find Ab."

He nodded, thinking to himself, only half hearing her.

"Why?" Gaby asked. "Why after all these years? You were part of Project Far-Star—you were one of the cosmonauts yourself—you didn't need to get mixed up in our troubles."

"Your troubles are the world's troubles," said Rafe. "They're also the troubles of the Project."

"Of the Project? The Project to put men out to Alpha Centauri and beyond?" There was disbelief in her voice.

"The Project's been hung up for nearly three years," said Rafe bluntly. "Going no place. The plan depends on an adaptation of cryonics—near-freezing the cosmonauts so as to slow down their life processes and extend their shipboard lifetimes. We'd have one on duty and three cooled at all times—that was the idea. But keeping the human body at low temperatures that long has turned out to cause nerve damage."

"I didn't know that." Gaby was watching him. They sped along in silence for a moment through the still-moonlit farm country.

"It's very top secret," Rafe said dryly.

"But what's it got to do with me—and Ab?"

"Ab's work has been pointing the way to literal, artificially induced hibernation for humans—without any freezing or drugs—for some time. I suggested him to the

Project three years ago, but a screening committee turned down the idea of trying to hire him. Three days ago I got at the files of that committee's action, and it was a washout."

"Washout?"

"They decided against Ab for no good reason," said Rafe. "They talked around the subject of what he could do for the Project, instead of ever really discussing it, then registered a vote of five to one against hiring him, on the basis that there was no clear evidence he could be useful—a nice, vague turndown."

"I still don't understand," said Gaby.

"Someone rigged that committee result," said Rafe. "Someone wanted Ab turned down—didn't want him on the Project. And the only reason for that could be that someone was afraid that if he joined the Project, we'd actually get a ship off to one of the far stars. In not too pretty a word—sabotage."

Gaby shook her head.

"That doesn't make sense," she said. "Who has anything to gain by keeping an interstellar ship from being launched?"

"Martin Pu-Li, perhaps," said Rafe. "The Project Head, for one. Once interstellar ships start going out, the research and development end of the Project, which is his baby, would stop being the most important and would become secondary to the actual cosmonaut and launching programs. Only, it doesn't have to be him. Someone else, people from Earth, could have got at that committee, too, through letters, phone calls—even through VIP visits, which we get every so often."

"But who on Earth—"

"Like Martin," Rafe said. "The men interested in maintaining the *status quo*. Pao Gallot. Bill Forebringer."

"Pao Gallot?" Gaby frowned. "Ab always talked about him as a completely dedicated man."

"Too dedicated, maybe," said Rafe. "As long as his Core Tap power stations run the factories that barely keep Earth from starving to death, he's the most important man in the world. Open up star routes so that even a few people have a hope of escaping the situation here and his importance is bound to be cut down somewhat."

"Not much."

"No. Not much," admitted Rafe. "But Pao, Martin, and Forebringer are as close as fingers on the same hand. And Forebringer, of course, only has the police powers he has as an emergency measure until the food problem is licked some way. For my money—and I've had more than a year now to watch things and think about them—it could be any or all of them who don't want anything changed and are ready to sabotage the Project or kidnap people like Ab to prevent it—"

He broke off suddenly.

"You never did tell me exactly how Ab was taken," he said to her.

"I don't really know if he was—actually taken, that is," Gaby said. "I mean, he may have gone voluntarily, but that's hard to believe. I told you how he spent hours the night before with Lucas, and you saw how Lucas can't or won't tell us what happened then. But, Lucas—tell Rafe what happened the next morning, when I was asleep and the men came for Ab."

"Ab told me to hide," said Lucas. "He said to stay out of sight of the men who came, so I did. I stayed in the kitchen when they came to the door."

"How many men were there?" Rafe asked.

"Two," said Lucas.

"Ordinary men? Not shadows like we fought earlier tonight at the house?"

"Two men with smell."

"They came to the door," Rafe said. "Ab answered the door?"

"Yes," said Gaby. "It was early morning—you remember I told you on the phone. I was still upstairs. I heard the door and voices, but I didn't think anything of it because it was daylight."

"Then what, Lucas?" Rafe asked the wolf.

"Ab talked. They talked. At the front door."

"What did they talk about?"

For a moment it did not seem that Lucas was going to answer. Then he spoke.

"Forever," he said.

Rafe turned, leaving the car to the autopilot alone. He looked at Lucas.

"Forever?" he echoed.

"Forever," answered Lucas. "Other things, but several times the two men said 'forever.' Once Ab said it. Then he went away with them, and closed the door behind them. I heard them drive away."

Rafe looked once more at Gaby.

"Maybe it wasn't an actual kidnaping, after all," he said. "Maybe Ab wanted to go, for some reason."

"No," said Lucas from the back. "He was sad to go. He hated the men who came. I smelled that on him."

"H'm-m," said Rafe. He thought for a moment and then turned to Gaby. "And no message? He didn't leave any word for you to find after he was gone?"

"Just that we were to go with you if you came," said Gaby. "To trust you."

Rafe did not start. But he looked slowly and searchingly at her.

"You don't think we'd have gone off with you just like that," Gaby said, "if Ab hadn't said something?"

"I guess not," said Rafe. "So, not only the six other men—Ab knew I was coming too?" He shot the word at her. "How?"

"I . . . don't know," she said. She was sitting back against the far door of the two-wheeler as far from him as possible. From the back seat came the faint, throaty warning of a growl. Rafe made himself relax, in body and voice.

"Maybe," said Gaby, "the Old Man told him."

He considered her closely.

"You really believe in this Old Man business, do you?" he said.

"Not really . . . or at least not before Ab said he'd talked to him." Her eyes were bright. "I didn't even hear the name until about a year or so ago. You know we've lived awfully quietly here. Four years ago Ab got this continuing grant from the Basic Science Foundation for his research, with the only condition being he teach one class a week at the college. We hardly knew anyone to talk to, so probably we were the last to hear about the Old Man. Of course, we knew about zombies right from the beginning—"

She laughed suddenly.

"Naturally, come to think of it," she said. "We were zombies ourselves—thanks to Ab. He and I and Lucas."

"Thanks to Ab?" Rafe asked. "None of you had natural immunity to the broadcasts?"

"I"—she frowned—"don't think so. I don't exactly remember. I think Ab started working on me as soon as I came home from the hospital after my accident. Of course, Lucas was one of Ab's experimental animals to begin with. Ab got him when he was only a few weeks old—you should have seen him as a cub!"

"So Ab began work on you after you came back from the hospital?" echoed Rafe thoughtfully. "Do you remember anything about the broadcasts while you were still in the hospital?"

She sat for a second, saying nothing. Suddenly she shuddered.

"Yes," she said. "I remember now. Nightmares."

"What kind of nightmares?"

"I—" She did not finish the sentence. "I don't remember exactly. But it wasn't what was in the nightmares, it was the *difference*. The difference between here and there —between the real world and what it was like while dreaming."

She shook herself slightly, as if to shrug off the memory.

"After I was home, Ab told me always to sleep in the daytime. Never to try to sleep while the broadcasts were on," she said. "And he trained us to resist the broadcast and stay awake."

"Did he say why you shouldn't sleep?"

"It was something—" She frowned. "Yes, that was it. It was something to do with vulnerability. Just as he thought my individual brain-wave pattern had been heavily damaged by the broadcasts while I was unconscious in the wreck, he thought anyone could be slightly damaged if he was in natural sleep during the broadcasts. So, I gave up sleeping nights. So did he. And Lucas."

"What did Ab say about the zombies?" Rafe asked. "Did he have any idea how they got their natural immunity?"

"He didn't think there was any such thing as a *natural* immunity," she said. "He pointed out that there was no such thing as zombie animals or birds who showed an immunity to the broadcast. He believed everyone, from the basic sleepwalker type on up to a zombie who could drive a car and get around and do purposeful things during the broadcast hours, was either a person who had been consciously trained to control the alpha-wave pattern of his brain or a person who had unconsciously trained himself to it."

Suddenly she turned her head to look full in his face.

"How about you?" she said. "You show a real immunity, and Ab hadn't worked on you. What makes you immune?"

"Ab's probably right," Rafe said. "I read up on the zombies and the broadcast effect on the brain-wave patterns as soon as I heard about it—and I've always had a chip on my shoulder when it came to someone else seeming to do something I couldn't. What I read led me to yoga, and I worked with that for a while. So you could say I'm both consciously and unconsciously self-trained, in Ab's terms."

"Pretty effectively self-trained, I'd say," she said. "You get around as if it were easy."

"Don't fool yourself," he said. "When I move, it's like wading through a heavy surf; and if I let myself go, I'd be asleep in ten seconds."

"But the way you fought back at the house, when you and Lucas fought those shadows or whatever I couldn't see," said Gaby. "You didn't look then like you were wading through heavy surf."

"Remember, our perceptions are slowed too," said Rafe. But he frowned. "Still, come to think of it, there's more to it than just that. For some reason, twice now, when I thought I was fighting for my life, I seemed to get free of the effect of the broadcasts . . ."

He described the fight with the two zombies at the street repair site, and the thrumming that had been inside him since he had come into the broadcast area, except during the two violent moments at the repair site and at the house.

"It could be body adrenalin has something to do with counteracting the influence," he said. "But that doesn't make much sense, because adrenalin's a stimulant and you saw how I reacted to the dexedrine. On the other hand, the Scotch, which is a depressant because of the alcohol in it, seems to help this thrumming feeling . . ."

He felt worse the minute he mentioned it. They had been driving for some time now, and the padding effect of the Scotch he had drunk before leaving the house was almost gone. He had been ignoring the thrumming, but now that he mentioned it, he seemed to feel it shaking him apart inside.

"I should have thought to bring some along," he said through teeth set against the interior discomfort. "It's like the old aspirin and hot-toddy cure for an asthmatic attack. No reason it should help, but it does. You don't feel the thrumming—like that?"

"No," said Gaby, turning to the back seat. "Lucas, pass me my bag."

Lucas dipped his head and a second later slid the small overnight bag into the front seat. Gaby opened it up and took out a laboratory bottle filled with colorless liquid, its glass top secured with white adhesive tape.

"I didn't have much room, so I brought lab alcohol instead of a bottle of liquor," she said. "I thought you could cut it with water and make it go that much further." She hesitated. "It's been around for some weeks and picked up some water from the air. But it still must be about a hundred and eighty proof. You can't drink it the way it is. We'll have to find something to mix it with."

He consulted the map of the car's autolocator.

"There's a rest stop about ten miles ahead at the side of the road," he said.

They pulled off the unlimited-speed strip and slowed down to coast at last off the road at the rest stop—a rustic area by the roadside with tight-locked doors on log-cabin-like buildings and a white-basined water fountain.

There were no cups. Rafe found a street map of Des Moines in the glove compartment of the car and folded it into a paper cup. He half-filled it from the fountain and took a gulp of the icy, iron-tasting water to moisten his mouth and throat first. Then he mixed another half-cup of the water with the lab alcohol.

Even diluted, it exploded like a bomb inside him when he tossed it down. For a minute he stood breathing heavily through mouth and nose, and then they all got back into the two-wheeler. Five minutes later they were once more on the unlimited-speed strip, headed north, and the thrumming was being muffled within him.

Twenty minutes after that they passed the Iowa-Minnesota border, but the sky to the east was graying.

"We're not going to make the Canadian border by daylight," Rafe said. "And we don't dare cross except when the broadcast's on. We'll try for Duluth and hole up for the day."

With the easing of the thrumming, Rafe's mind began to wake and work again, slowly—because of the combined effects of the alcohol and the power broadcast—but certainly.

He lost himself in thought as they hummed, around the Twin Cities and headed north along the Lake Superior-Mississippi canal toward Duluth. Overhead the sky was growing steadily brighter. About ten miles short of Duluth they slowed, moved over across the lower-speed strips, and pulled off at last at the side of the road.

"We'll wait until a little after sunrise," he said, "then go on in, find a motel, and say we had to spend the night by the side of the road when the broadcast time caught up with us."

They found a minor motel on North Shore Drive of the harbor city. Lucas lay quietly under a blanket on the floor of the rear seat of the two-wheeler while Rafe signed Gaby and himself in as Mr. and Mrs. Albert Nyisem from Ames, Iowa.

"The broadcast time caught up with us, just twenty miles south of town," said Rafe, yawning. "It's no fun sleeping in a car."

"I guess not," said the motel manager, a thick, fifty-year-old man with a tight smile and sharp eyes. "Every so often I see people like you come in who got caught. I suppose you want to get some decent sleep now in real beds?"

"How right you are," said Rafe.

"Don't worry about a thing, then," said the manager. "Just hang the don't disturb sign out on your doorknob, and I'll tell the maid not to bother you. Sleep as late as you like and don't worry about a thing."

"Thanks," said Rafe.

He drove the car around the motel to the cottage with the number matching that of the key he had been given. A couple of cottages down, another couple was just pulling out. As soon as they were gone, Rafe smuggled Lucas into their own cottage. Gaby had already carried in her bag and drawn the various drapes and blinds over the windows.

"What now?" she asked, as Rafe put the Do Not

DISTURB sign on the outside of the door, closed it, and shot the bolt inside.

"Now we get some rest," he said. "I'll pay for a second night, but before dark we'll take off again and get out of sight of anyone by the time dark comes and the local broadcast starts. Tonight we ought to make Nipigon. Then it's a case of tracing those zombies who were waiting for me at the street repair spot. If we can make a connection there, it shouldn't take long to find out who sent them, and who's got Ab. There aren't that many zombies in the world to make a long chain of command from whoever's in charge to the men who were waiting for me at your place."

She nodded, took her bag, and went into the bathroom of the motel. Rafe lay down, still fully clothed, on one of the twin beds in the room and pulled over him a blanket that was lying folded at the bottom of the bed. He was instantly asleep. . . .

He awoke, abruptly, to a hammering on the door. Gaby, wearing a white nightgown, was sitting up in the other bed with the sheets and blankets half covering her. Lucas stood silent, but rigid, on the carpet in the center of the room, facing the door.

"Police!" shouted a voice outside. "Open up, here!"

The door was already cracked from its top edge halfway down to the door handle, as if those outside had tried to break in without warning—before finding the additional lock of the closed bolt barring their way.

Rafe slid out of bed.

"Lucas," he whispered. "They mustn't know you're in existence. Come on." Lucas hesitated. "Didn't Ab tell you to hide when the other men came?"

Lucas turned and followed Rafe as he ran to the bathroom at the back of the motel and stepped into it. The room had one window, high in a wall to the right of the washstand—a small window, but one Lucas might squeeze through.

"Out here, Lucas," whispered Rafe, throwing the window open, the sound of its rising lost in the renewed hammering on the front door. He unhooked the screen and swung it wide.

Lucas made one leap to the washstand. Rafe caught and steadied the wolf's surprisingly heavy body as Lucas's claws slipped on the slick surface of the bowl.

"Stay hidden," Rafe said. "Find us after dark. Then, do what you can. Now, go—"

He pushed, almost threw Lucas through the opening. The wolf vanished into daylight. Rafe hastily hooked the screen and ran back to open the front door just before it disintegrated under the pounding it was receiving.

"What's this all about—"

"You're under arrest," said the first of several policemen to surround him. "Both of you."

Rafe felt handcuffs closing on his wrists as his hands were pulled behind him. He was marched out to a police three-wheeler and pushed into its rear seat. A moment later Gaby, with a blanket wrapped around her and her overnight bag in her hand, was pushed in beside him. The motel owner stuck his head in the door of the police car.

"You thought I wouldn't know?" the motel owner said. "Didn't I say I'd seen people coming in after they'd been caught out on the road by the broadcast? After a night in the car they'd be half dead and stumbling around—"

"That's all right," said a policeman, shoving past him and sitting down in the back seat with Rafe and Gaby. "You did your duty and checked with us. Now, forget it."

"Took you long enough to get here—" the motel operator began to the policeman, but the latter closed the car door in his face.

They drove off. It was, Rafe saw, late afternoon. He and Gaby must have slept like dead people. When they reached the jail they were separated, and Rafe found himself put in a room with no bars on the single, ground-floor window and with what looked like a hospital bed in one corner of the white-painted room.

"Strip," said the policeman who brought Rafe in, handing him a hospital gown. "Put this on."

"What—" Rafe began.

"Just strip," said the policeman. "Put on the gown."

Rafe obeyed, and the policeman carried Rafe's clothes out of the room. Outside the window, the day was waning fast.

Three more policemen entered, followed by a man wearing a white jacket. Without warning, the three threw themselves on Rafe and pinned him down on his back on the bed.

"What is this?" cried Rafe, caught by surprise, helpless

in their grasp. The man in the white jacket approached him with a hypodermic syringe.

"His right arm, above the elbow, there," said the man in white.

"Answer me! What're you doing to me?"

"Standard treatment for zombies," grunted one of the policemen as Rafe made a surge of effort to avoid the approaching needle. "You're going to sleep through the night, brother, whether you want to or not—just like the rest of us normal folk."

The needle went in. Into Rafe's mind flashed the memory of what Gaby had reported Ab as saying—that there was danger to the individual's brain-wave pattern in being normally asleep during the broadcasts, and serious danger in being involuntarily unconscious at that time.

But there was nothing he could do about it now. The needle went in and was withdrawn. Cautiously, the policemen let him go.

"That should hold him," said the man in the white jacket, stepping away from the bed. "I gave him enough to hold him for twenty-four hours—easily enough to keep him under until the UN Marshal gets here."

Already, Rafe could feel the drug taking hold, like a soft hand enfolding and stopping the machinery of his mind. His tongue was going numb.

7

As if at some great distance, he heard the door to his room closing behind the policemen and the white-suited man. With a massive effort he turned the great weight of his head with reluctant neck muscles so that he gazed toward the window. The light still filled the sky. He could not see the sun from where he was, but it could not be quite down. He had a few minutes, anyway —maybe more than a few minutes—to do whatever could be done before the broadcast came on to add its soporific influence to the effect of whatever sedative or narcotic they had given him.

But even as he thought this, the drug was taking hold and blurring his mind so that he could not think, pulling him under. In the end, he went down with it, into unconsciousness, or something like it. . . .

At first it was only like drowning. But a dry and stifled drowning in which his whole body was held paralyzed, so that he could not struggle or call out. After a while, however, this passed and he became conscious again, but conscious only to the point of being aware that he was dreaming or hallucinating.

It seemed to him that he was in something like a series of very dimly lit rooms or caverns so far underground that he would die of old age before he could ever reach the surface, even if he could find his way out. The rooms were full of discarded, destroyed, and broken things and with an oppressive atmosphere that transmitted the emotional, rather than the physical, feeling of his being at the center of all possible pressures.

It was as if he were buried at the center of a universe. A different universe, he thought—but all the things around him rustled and whispered and hurried to assure him that this was the universe he had always known, but now being seen in its true appearance, stripped of all its decorations and paddings of illusory superstitions down to a stark hopelessness of truth.

The broken and discarded things came clustering around him, whispering at him to give up and agree, and he reached out for some sort of club or stick to beat them off. But everything he picked up broke or crumbled in his hand and was useless. Finally he ran, and for a little while he out-distanced them.

But he was conscious of the continuing pressure of something inimical—whatever it was that had been behind the things when they had tried to make him give up. He felt it somewhere nearby, and he found himself searching through the underground rooms for it. So he came after a while into a series of rooms where people were drinking, talking, and dancing, as if at a party; but all their talk was in whispers together, and stopped when he came up. Something within him told him that it would be useless to ask them questions—for he heard them sniggering behind his back once he had gone by, as if they knew what he searched for but were sure he could never find it.

Then, gradually, he became aware that they were all hollow, these people. Men and women alike, they had been scooped out from behind so that merely the front three-quarters of their skin and hair and clothes were left —just enough so that viewed from straight on they appeared to be in the round.

Gradually as he moved among them—and in spite of the fact that they were mostly very clever at keeping their faces and fronts toward him—he began to catch glimpses of the emptiness behind what was left, like the emptiness of a rock lobster tail once the meat had been taken out of it. Their whispering, heard all together like the sound of dry waves on a desiccated beach in utter darkness, was trying to tell him to give up, to abandon hope, just as had the broken things in the rooms he had passed through earlier.

Still, even as he ran from the corrosive chorus of their whispering, the illogical conviction formed in him that somewhere, even here, there was a firm weapon that would not crumble when he tried to use it—if he could only find it. And with one firm weapon he could prove them all wrong and defeat their universe. He had escaped from the hollow people now. He was in a series of barely lit caverns—true caverns rather than rooms now—through which he had to grope his way, but which held neither things nor the façades of people nor anything else but rock floor and empty stone walls arching to some high point overhead.

Then he found his enemy, the inimical creature behind the broken things and the hollow people, all alone by himself, or herself or itself, in one huge cavern. It crouched against one wall, for all its size—and it was many times bigger than he was—guarding a throne it had sat on once but had long since outgrown, like a mouse guarding a crumb.

He did not see it clearly, for though the cavern was lighted, the lights were so dim and far overhead and the shadows were so thick and black by the wall where it crouched that seeing was barely possible. But without seeing it clearly he understood it suddenly. Once it had been as human as himself, but now it had gradually increased to a gargantuan, abnormal size, like the swollen body of an old queen wasp among the smaller figures of the normal hive denizens.

Only in this case the growth had come about by the addition of body on top of overbody, shell upon shell, each one a rustling envelope of a dead year lived and lost to no purpose. Self-trapped at the core was what had once been a human being, but it was lost now and buried, not only in the dry and rustling years and years of its overbodies, but in its own belief that it was as monstrous as those overbodies made it. And in that belief it had constructed this universe where everything pressed inward to the center and that center was filled with broken things and hollow people.

He saw then that he should kill it—not only in his own self-defense, but in pity to release it from that existence which it had deluded itself was not a torment but a dark joy. He looked around and found nothing but a large and jagged stone; when he picked up the stone, it crumbled to dust in his hands.

"You see?" it that was imprisoned within its countless years husked at him with the rustlings of its dry overbodies—and the husked voice was like the whispering of the hollow people and the rustlings of the broken things, earlier. "Nothing here has any power to harm me. I am Satan."

"No," he said.

It rustled louder against the wall where it crouched, and moved as if to flow over him and stifle him in its dry envelopes of bodies.

"I am Satan!"

"Satan is nothing to me," he said, and all the time he was looking around for another stone, a broken stalactite, a rusty ax or sword to use.

"Satan is something to everyone!" it rustled. "Satan is beyond all pain. Satan is behind pain, past the point of being able to be hurt any more. Satan is death in life that never ends—forever and forever and forever . . ."

Then, while it was still talking, he found in quick succession an ancient spear, a two-headed ax, and a rusty, ancient revolver. But the spear shattered into splinters when he threw it, and the head of the ax flew off when he swung it—flew off and shattered against the rocky wall—and the revolver snapped its hammer uselessly on empty cylinders and broke apart in mid-air when he tried to throw it at the creature that called itself Satan.

"Give up," it said now. "Give up, give up, give up . . ."

Against his will, then, he felt his hope fading, his courage going. He tried desperately to remember an instance of hope. He did his best to summon up an image of courage, but nothing came.

"Come join yourself to me," rustled Satan. "Come live forever in death-in-life, adding your overbodies to mine. There is no more use trying, no more use searching, no more—"

And then, without warning, it came to him—the image of a real and solid knife with a leather handle and a blade of blue steel—and it sparked off inspiration.

"Lucas!" he called.

The rustling of the Satan rose to a roar, to a sound like a dry hurricane, as it tried to drown him out.

"No!" it rustled. And all its black hopelessness poured out upon him, trying to drown him before he could call again.

"Lucas!" He shouted desperately. "LUCAS!"

And Lucas came.

He came not as his ordinary self, but as a great, gaunt ghost-wolf, larger than an elephant—almost as large as the thing that called itself Satan—flickering all over with tiny blue flames that illumined him and lit up his yellow eyes. He came bounding, leaping into the cavern like a puppy at play, bearing in his mouth a tiny-looking knife with a black leather handle and a blue steel blade.

"Give me the knife, Lucas!"

Lucas crouched and howled, and the knife dropped tinkling on the rock at Rafe's feet. Then Lucas howled again and went back to leaping and playing with the rustling Satan-creature that backed and reared like some huge, papery slug, and spread itself against the ceiling until it was enormous enough to fall upon and bury both man and wolf.

And Rafe took up the knife by the point and threw it into the overhanging Satan-thing. It flew from his fingers like stone from a slingshot, straight into the huge, rustling body above them.

Satan screamed.

Snatching up Rafe in his jaws like a toy mouse in the jaws of a dog, Lucas sprang upward, brushing aside the falling body of Satan, springing right through the solid rock overhead as if it were mist. Up and up he sprang— but his jaws slipped, and Rafe went tumbling away from the wolf, back through the mist-rock, losing himself.

The rock began to solidify around him, closing in on him again, threatening to squeeze the life out of his body. It was like a great weight coming at him from all sides, but fury boiled up in him at the thought of being beaten, now, after what he had done. He batted the rock away from his face with a superhuman effort. . . .

And sat up. A moonlit room was around him. On a small, white-painted cabinet by his bed was a metal basin holding an empty hypodermic needle. Thrusting aside drug and broadcast effect together, he grabbed up the basin and threw it.

It shattered the window and disappeared into the night outside.

"Lucas!" he shouted hoarsely to that night behind the broken window, and fell back on the bed, the shadows closing in around him, shadows that were hardening into rock. And he was once more lost in the . . .

Lucas's jaws closed upon him. Carrying him once more. Lucas sprang upward. Up and up through the rock, until they burst at last through sea bottom into the depths of an ocean, and the wetness poured over Rafe, filling his mouth and nose and eyes, stinging like liquid fire . . .

He pulled himself upright, choking, wiping at his eyes.

He was soaked about the face and shoulders. After a moment he got his watering eyes clear enough to see the shaggy wolf head beside the bed on which he lay and a dark whisky bottle lying spilled on the blanket that had covered him.

Clumsily he grabbed up the bottle. It was about a third full.

"Nice work, Lucas," he said thickly. "But we'll save it for later. Right now they've got as much inside me as I can take."

He scrambled out of bed, fighting the inertia of his leaden body, but buoyed up by a blazing exultation inside him.

"Keep me out for twenty-four hours, he said," Rafe muttered, hearing his own words thick in his ear. "Didn't know the kind of dosage I can take . . . you heard me calling, did you, Lucas?"

"I heard you," said Lucas. "Now—Gabrielle."

Impatiently, the wolf moved toward the door of the room. Rafe went after him. His eyes and mouth were more comfortable now, but the inside of his nose still felt aflame from the spilled whisky Lucas had evidently tried to get inside him by any means. The door was not even locked. Man and wolf together, they stepped out into a pitch-dark corridor.

Rafe reached down and took hold of the thick fur at Lucas's neck.

"No light switch here," he said. "You guide me, Lucas—along the wall."

With Lucas leading, Rafe stumbled along the wall in the darkness, running his hand and forearm over it at switchplate height until he felt something bump and jar against his wrist as the wrist passed over it.

"Hold up. Back," he said to Lucas. He stopped, reached back at arm's length, and found the switch plate again. His fingers moved the stud—and light was all around them.

They stood in a long corridor leading to what was clearly the door for this wing or section of the building. They went forward, opened the door, and Rafe found another light switch. Beyond was plainly an office, with several doors opening off it.

"Where'll they have Gaby?" muttered Rafe to himself.

"I'll find her," Lucas said.

He went directly to one of the doors, rose on his hind legs, and turned the knob with his jaws. The door pushed open. Beyond was darkness. Rafe, following close behind the wolf, reached out and found another light switch, and a second later they were looking down a corridor just like the one onto which Rafe's room had opened.

Lucas ran to one of the doors, rose on his hind legs, and opened it. By the time Rafe followed and found the light switch, Lucas was already up with his front legs on the bed, licking the unmoving face of an unconscious Gaby and whining softly. Her tubelike vehicle stood at the foot of the bed.

"They doped her up, too," said Rafe thickly. "And even if I knew what they used, I wouldn't dare monkey around with an antidote, the way people seem to react unnaturally under the broadcast influence. Let's just get her out of here and as far away as possible, Lucas."

It was nearly impossible for Rafe to lift Gaby into the vehicle, still fighting against the double influence of the drug and the broadcast as he was. But finally he got her into it, wedged her overnight bag in with her, activated the cylinder's controls, and floated her out to the office section.

"Wait, now," he said, halting. "We've got to get a car, someplace."

"Down below," said Lucas. "A lot of cars. I can smell them."

Some search turned up an elevator which dropped them to a parking garage under the building. The garage was filled with police cars, but there were a few civilian models. None of these had the keys in them. But Lucas, following his nose, found a board hanging in a small office at the back of the garage with a number of keys on it—and his nose identified the key belonging to the car Rafe picked. Next to the board was a row of lockers. The fifth one down yielded civilian clothes of about Rafe's size. He put these on, and with the key returned to the car. The automatic doors of the garage unlocked and opened before them as they drove up to them, and minutes later they were on North Shore Drive, headed toward the Canadian border.

The border was nothing but two dark, locked station buildings, one U.S., one Canadian, past which they traveled without even slowing down. They wheeled north

past Fort William and Port Arthur and swung into the
dark, still-small town of Nipigon as the control-board
clock in their car showed a little less than two hours re-
maining before sunrise.

As they reached the edge of the town, Rafe slowed pre-
cipitously. There was a small rustle from the back seat
where they had laid Gaby, followed by Gaby's voice saying, "Oh!"

A second later she spoke again.

"Where am I?"

Rafe risked one quick glance back over his shoulder.
She was sitting up. He pulled the car to a halt at the side
of the street and then turned about. Lucas was already
over the back of the front seat where he had ridden with
Rafe, and beside Gaby, trying to lick her face.

"Lucas, stop it!" She pushed the wolf back. "Where are
we?"

"How do you feel?" Rafe asked.

"All right," she said. "Why shouldn't—oh, I remember.
They were going to give me some kind of injection."

"Didn't they?" Rafe asked.

"I guess they did." She felt the upper part of her left
arm. "Yes, it's sore. But that's one of the things Ab was
training me to handle as part of training me to use my
legs again. In case of anything that might make me unconscious again while a broadcast was on, I immediately went
into a special state of brain-wave pattern in which the
broadcast couldn't affect me and all the natural defenses
of my body were mobilized against whatever had made
me unconscious. It seems to have handled whatever they
shot me with."

He looked at her curiously.

"How did Ab work with you?" he asked.

"The same way he worked with Lucas and the other
experimental animals," she answered. "He did a lot of
brain-mapping of each individual. Then he charted what
he theorized were aberrations in that individual's pattern.
Then he blocked off the aberrant pattern if he could and
tried to replace it—override it if he couldn't block it out
—by training the individual to use another pattern."

"How'd he do this?" Rafe glanced at the odd shape of
Lucas's skull. "Electrodes into the brain at specific
points?"

"Not for the last few years," she said. "He used a short-range—very short-range—transmitting device, something like the powerful ones that transmit the power broadcasts. Though, of course, the power broadcasts are just crude, massive spoutings of energy, and his little machine was highly selective and variable."

"In that case," he said, "why does Lucas have—"

"That device on his head?" she answered. "Lucas is a special case. A wolf hasn't any natural speech center in his brain, like a human has. Ab had to build a mechanical one for him. That's it on his skull. You can't see it, but he's also got an artificial larynx, and artificial vocal cords as well, with a special attachment to take the place of the work human lips and mouth do—otherwise he couldn't make understandable sounds, even with the speech center."

Rafe whistled softly in admiration.

"Actually," Gaby went on, "Lucas still doesn't *speak* in the sense that we do. He has a microcomputer surgically implanted at the base of his skull. What happens is that his brain's electrical activities key off certain speech patterns, and these patterns select prerecorded speech impulses from the computer which are fed to the artificial voice mechanisms in his throat area. That's why you can sometimes ask him something and get no answer at all. It's because you've asked for something his computer section isn't programmed to supply—even if he actually knows the answer himself."

Rafe frowned sharply.

"You mean Lucas could know some things we need to know right now, and still not be able to tell us?" he demanded.

"Why, yes. That's what I was telling you—" Gaby broke off suddenly. "Of course! I'm so used to taking his not answering for granted I forgot how much difference it might make to us right now—"

She interrupted herself again and turned to Lucas, who was sitting on the back seat of the car beside her.

"Lucas," she said, "do you really know where Ab is? Do you really know, but can't tell us?"

The wolf whined and tried to lick her face. She fended him off and then petted him.

"We'll find him," said Lucas. "Then I can kill."

"Well?" asked Rafe from the front seat. "Do you think he knows?"

"I'm . . . not sure," she said. "There's no reason I can think of he couldn't give us a straight yes or no to that question. Unless Ab deliberately conditioned him not to say."

"That last night before he disappeared you said he had Lucas in the lab for several hours . . ."

She nodded.

"Yes, he could have done something like that then."

"Well," Rafe turned back to the controls. "Whichever it is, we've only got a couple of hours left until daylight. Let's see if we can locate this Crazian's Corner before then."

"Crazian's Corner?"

"Don't you remember?" he said, putting the car back into motion. "The service slip I found in the car with the Ontario license plates and the two zombies from the road repair spot."

"Oh, yes. I remember now—" Her voice took on a faintly worried note. "Rafe, you don't think the broadcast damaged me after all, while I was lying there in the police station drugged?"

"No," he said. But, to himself, he was not so sure. . . .

They found a roadside public telephone and looked up Crazian's Corner in the local phone book. The address given was 4023 Manchester Drive, which turned out, when they reached it, to be a small complex of vehicle service center, restaurant, grocery, and disposable garment shop.

Rafe broke the glass of the service center door. An alarm bell began to clang. Ignoring it, he opened the door and let them inside. More because it was annoying than for any other reason, he located the inside wires to the shouting alarm high on an outside wall of the building, and snapped them. The noise ceased.

He turned up the lights inside the center and began to hunt for the sales-receipt file. By the time he had located it in a drawer of a desk in the center's small office, Gaby and Lucas had found the door to the adjoining restaurant and gone through it. Rafe pawed through the receipts, which were arranged by date, and after a while discovered one that matched the flimsy slip he had taken from the car of the two zombies at the street repair in Grinnell. The customer's signature on the seller's copy was just barely legible. It was Darrell Hasken. He turned to the local phone book and found a Darrell Hasken listed.

He went to get Gaby and Lucas, but as he stepped through into the restaurant, the delicious odor of frying bacon and eggs surrounded him.

"Hungry?" called Gaby from behind the counter, upright in her vehicle.

He was starved.

They were all starved. It was another twenty minutes before they had finished eating. They went back through to the service center and out the door where he had broken in. Outside the sky was paling, but the shadows were still thick on the ground—so that he did not see their attackers until these were actually upon them. There were more of them this time, full men, not shadows, and they moved with more facility and speed than the zombies he had yet encountered.

He heard Gaby screaming and the snarl of Lucas rising over the shouts of the attackers. Then something like a heavy cloth was wrapped about him and stifled him into unconsciousness.

8

The next thing Rafe knew, he was seated in an aircraft capable of holding perhaps twelve passengers, and with that awareness began a peculiar period in which he was not completely in control of himself.

The aircraft was flying at a great height. The three times Rafe summoned up the energy to look out the window beside his seat, he saw first an endless expanse of water, then a landscape of ice and snow, and finally barren-looking plains, rising to a range of mountains dead ahead.

He found he could not work up any immediate concern or alarm about his situation. It was not as if he had been drugged. It was rather as if he were mentally isolated in a warm cocoon of indifference. As long as he made no effort to move or think, he sat quite comfortably in something like a pleasantly absent-minded state. But even the desire to move his head and look out the window seemed to require a massive effort.

He made that effort again, to look across the aisle of the aircraft at the seat opposite him. Gaby sat in it, gazing straight ahead with a placid expression. Lucas was nowhere to be seen.

Rafe turned his head to look forward again himself—the return movement was easy, effortless—and withdrew back into his cocoon. With his gaze front, he could see his hands lying open on his knees. He was not tied or secured in any way except for this compulsion which made doing and thinking nothing infinitely easier than movement and thought.

He sat, nonthinking.

After a little while he became vaguely conscious of a faintly nagging sensation in the back of his mind—the same sort of nagging sensation that afflicts someone who has just left home and is vaguely troubled by the thought of something forgotten or not done.

The feeling continued. It was like a small animal gnawing away at him below the platform level of the indifference that held him. Gradually, without realizing exactly how he had come to realize it, he woke to the fact that the small, gnawing uneasiness was a part of his mind which was somehow below, behind, or out of reach of whatever held the rest of him in a cocoon of indifference; and it was struggling against the effect of that indifference on the rest of his mind.

He watched the activity of this small uneasiness for some while, as the aircraft bored silently through the upper atmosphere. As he continued to watch, its image sharpened. It was, he saw, that instinctive part of him which had never been able to admit that others could do something he could not. That element of him which was not capable of accepting defeat.

It could not accept now the fact that he was being held physically and mentally inactive against his will. It insisted on trying to struggle. As his own feeling of it became clearer, there gradually seeped into his upper mind the concept that possibly he could carry on his thinking on this lower level where the nagging lived, without interference from what was holding him captive.

He tried it.

It was a strange way to think, he found. It required pure thought—thought without the color of emotion, without the concrete imagery of words or symbols.

His own will and intent, considered this way, were a bundle of forces; against them, at the moment, another force was being applied to immobilize him. This other force was turning his own strength back upon himself. He recognized the outside force then, by an intuitive, spark-gaplike mental jump, as a broadcast similar to the power broadcasts that enforced slumber on the world during its dark hours. Only this was a broadcast that was more selective, inhibiting thought and movement without putting him to sleep.

However—intuition sparked again in him below the level of conscious thought—if he could resist the ordinary power broadcasts, then this transmission also ought to be something he could resist—if he could only identify the pattern of its attack and work around it.

Below the level of conscious thought, his mind began to wake and move about, feeling its strength on this lower level like a sleeping giant roused after a lifetime of slumber.

Everything that could be done on a conscious level could be done here as well, he saw—but in different terms. It was as if the language of his thought had been forced to change from algebra to calculus. The two languages were apparently completely dissimilar, but they were joined together in the root that was himself.

In fact, maybe he could do more with the calculus of thought than he had formerly been able to do with the algebra of it. He explored, feeling about like a blind man, with this lower level of his mind, and felt Gaby's mind, close by, but unaware of his.

He felt out for Lucas—and came up hard against the live and burning identity that was the wolf. Lucas, it seemed, thought more on this level than on the conscious, human level which was alien to him.

Lucas was not with them on the aircraft.

"Why not?" Silently, the lower mind of Rafe formed the question.

"Ab told me to hide when the men came who took him away," Lucas answered, at once from a great distance and from no distance at all. "You told me to run and hide from the motel in the city last night. When you and Gabrielle were both unconscious and I saw I could not win, I got away, instead, and hid."

"Where are you now?" asked Rafe mentally, meaning, Where is your physical body now? because all that was nonphysical of Lucas was right beside him on the aircraft at that moment.

"Near where they caught us," Lucas answered. "A little way from there is the edge of the town we were in, and beyond that edge are the woods—the north woods where I was whelped. In the woods I'm safe."

"Are you hurt, Lucas?"

Amazingly, like an invisible whirlpool, the air just in front of Rafe's eyes seemed to spin and thicken into an image of the wolf's mask. Lucas looked into his eyes from a distance of less than a foot.

"No," said Lucas.

"I can see you, Lucas."

"I can see you," the mind of Lucas replied. "I can't see

Gabrielle, but I can feel she's all right—only she's something like sleeping."

"She's all right," Rafe thought. "Lucas, tell me. Can you see Ab?"

"No."

"Can you feel Ab the same way you can feel Gabrielle?"

"Yes."

"Do you know where Ab is?"

"Yes. No," said Lucas. "I can feel Ab out there, somewhere, but where there is, I don't know. But we will find him."

"What makes you so sure?"

"Ab promised me we would find him."

Rafe thought for a while, considering the situation with the unfamiliar calculus of his lower thoughts.

"Can you tell me, Lucas," he thought, "are we—Gaby and I and the rest of us on this plane—going toward where Ab is now?"

"No," said Lucas promptly. "Ab's not the way you're going. He's off another way."

"How can I find him?"

"A man knows a man knows a man knows."

"I don't understand," Rafe said.

"A man who knows a man who knows a man who knows."

The last two statements of Lucas's did not fit the calculus of Rafe's lower mind. Rafe mentally tried them in several different patterns—and then suddenly realized what the difficulty was. Lucas was, like himself, thinking on the asymbolic lower level of the mind, but the question Rafe had asked had only been answerable in the symbolic words fed to the wolf by the implanted microcomputer of his artificial speech mechanism.

It was as if Rafe had asked the chemical nature of a substance and the only way the answer could be given was in the terms of an inadequate and ancient alchemy.

"It's all right," he said to Lucas. "Stay where you are now. We'll come back for you."

"Yes," said Lucas. "You'll come back for me. Meanwhile, no one else can find me. I'll wait."

The image of the wolf face faded from Rafe's vision. He turned his attention back to the aircraft and those in it.

He could feel the presence of the others aboard now,

as he had felt the presence of Lucas. There were eight of them on the aircraft, and, surprisingly, all except the two men at the controls seemed to be under some variation of the same sort of transmitted pressure that was keeping him helpless in his seat.

Or was he helpless in his seat?

He had met the problem of the power broadcasts by retraining his mind and body to operate under an enforced pattern of electrical activity of his brain that normally accompanied deep sleep. If he could retrain himself to operate in spite of one type of transmission, he ought to be able to retrain himself to operate in spite of another —this present one. He relaxed, letting his body sag back in the chair, and reached for that calm of mind which would be solid ground on which to stand while he operated.

Peace. Accept all; oppose nothing. Thus is victory invariably achieved over any and all opposing forces.

I am who I am . . . who I am . . . who I am. I . . . I . . . I . . . and none other . . . I and none other . . . I . . .

An hour or so later, the aircraft began to descend, halted in mid-air, and made the final stages of descent vertically. As it touched ground, Rafe felt his conscious control of his body slide like a hand out of one glove and into another—where he was suddenly free. He glanced about. No one was looking.

Experimentally, he made an effort to rise from his seat. His muscles responded without struggle. There was no longer any effective opposition from the pressure of the pattern being transmitted to him.

He sat back in his seat and waited. He was still aware of the pattern that had been controlling him. Shortly, he felt it pushing him to stand and leave the aircraft. He stood as if it still controlled him. The others about him were also standing. Together they left the plane.

They stepped out into sunlight, but almost immediately, a shadow replaced the light. Glancing up, he saw it was the shadow of an almost vertical cliff of reddish granite, into which the metal pad where their aircraft had landed was being withdrawn like a tongue back into its mouth. A moment later, aircraft and passengers alike were inside the wall of rock, and a vertical door was sliding down to cover the massive slot, a hundred feet wide and thirty feet high, through which they had been carried.

Within were passageways and rooms cut out of the rock, and they were brightly lit, so large in area and lofty-ceilinged that they seemed more like the streets and open places of a city than anything else. One of the pilots of the aircraft, holding a small green box in his hand about the size of a pound of butter, started off down one of the passageways. Gaby had already been helped back into her personal vehicle. She slid along after him without a word, and Rafe also followed.

The pilot led them to a double suite of smaller rooms. Gaby went off, still without talking, into the right-hand cluster of rooms. The pilot followed her. Rafe went to the left and sought out the bathroom of that particular room-group.

He had not shaved for more than two days, or showered. The face that looked back at him out of the mirror above the washstand in the bathroom was as wild looking as the wolf mask of Lucas. He found depilatory, soap, and towels, and spent the best part of the next hour making himself human again.

There was not much he could do about his clothes. He checked the closets in the rooms of his half of the double suite, in hopes that perhaps something had been provided for him to wear. But the closets were almost sterile in their emptiness.

He went into the other set of rooms and found Gaby also cleaned up, out of her vehicle, and lying on top of the covers of her bed. She gave him a smile that was almost a grin as he entered.

"How do you feel?" she asked.

"Fine," he said. "Oh, I could use some sleep, but that's a need I'm used to. How do you feel?"

For answer, she grinned again, reached under the small of her back—and pulled out the green box their guide had been carrying. A second grope beneath her produced a thick fold of cloth, which, when she opened it, revealed rows of small hand tools fitted through loops in the cloth.

She touched her ear, and pointed warningly at the ceiling of the room. Rafe nodded. Obviously, the room would be bugged with listening devices. But how had Gaby gotten her hands on the green control box?

"The man that brought us both here," she went on, in a casual, conversational tone, taking something that looked like a small screw driver to the box, "was good enough to wait around until I got cleaned up, and then he helped me out of my cart onto the bed, here. I don't think he realized how much of a load I am. He had to put down across the room there what he was carrying"—she pointed at the box in her hand—"to get me out of the cart and into the bed."

So. Gaby had picked the man's pocket as he lifted her into the bed. Before Rafe's eyes the little screw-driverlike instrument found some invisible seam in the box. Its top popped off. Inside was a mass of circuits.

"I almost hated to ask him to carry me like that," Gaby went on, reaching for something like a thin pick, with which she probed among the circuits of the box. "But I'd gotten so used to Ab helping me. Did you know I used to work with Ab in the lab until all hours of the night, and I'd be so tired I could hardly help when he lifted me out of my cart?"

"Is that so?" said Rafe. His eyes were on the tight mass of circuitry inside the box. It made no sense to him, but Gaby's pick was moving expertly from point to point inside it.

"Yes," she said, laying down the pick and putting the top of the box back on. "Ab felt guilty about working me like that. But he was really a pure theoretician. I was the mechanic around the place."

She replaced the pick and the screw-driverlike tool in their loops and rolled up the cloth container. She handed it, together with the green box, to Rafe.

"Of course," she said, pointing to her vehicle, "it helped that I had my cart fixed up to carry most of what I needed when I worked with him." She pointed again to the vehicle.

Rafe stepped over to the vehicle and looked down inside it. Some little distance below the top rim, he saw a row of cloth pockets with button-down flaps. One flap was unbuttoned. He lifted the flap, found the pocket empty and slid the small package of tools into it, then buttoned it again. He turned to Gaby, hefting the green box in his hand, and raised his eyebrows, questioningly.

She pointed across the room to a small table near the entrance door. He took the box to the table.

"It would've been much easier if I could get around without my cart, of course," she said. "Ab kept hoping he could get me back to walking again. But it was no use. I was helpless without my cart. I couldn't even take a step or two on my own—let alone walk clear across the lab, which was the first goal he set for us."

There was the unmistakable note of a hidden meaning in her last words. Rafe set the green box down on the small table. He looked back at the bed on which Gaby lay and measured the space with his eyes from the bed to the table that now held the box. She nodded vigorously. The distance was a good thirty feet. Clearly, Gaby was giving him some idea of the distance she could cover without her cart. Apparently she was able to walk a good deal more than he had realized. He nodded back—message understood.

"You've got to keep trying," said Rafe, aloud. "You never know. It's just a matter of understanding what makes things work."

"I've got a pretty good idea already," Gaby answered. Her eyes sparkled. "You'd be surprised at what I can do if I have to. Maybe you'd better go get some of that sleep you said you wanted. No telling when somebody may come to get us for something. For all we know, that man that brought us here could come back at any time."

"I suppose you're right," said Rafe. "He might just remember he forgot to tuck you in. Or something."

"Or something," she said. Both their eyes went to the green box sitting on the table near the door, thirty feet from where a supposedly half-paralyzed girl lay unable to move from her bed. Rafe gave her a smile, a little salute, and went out.

He went back to the bed in his section of rooms and lay down. He was asleep instantly, and for some time there were fleeting intervals of unconnected, normal dreams—and then, without warning, he was back in the caverns at the center of the universe.

He was in the same cavern where the creature that called itself Satan lived. But this time it had a different shape. It was a tower of burnt-out combustibles, as if from a countless number of fires that had been built one on top of the ashes of the previous one, so that it, or the being that called itself Satan, was a structure tall and lightless, at the very top of which the small flames of a last fire flickered distantly, high above the dark floor.

"Did you think you had killed me?" the being said to

Rafe. "Did you think you could get away? Nothing kills me, and every way you go will bring you back here—"

Rafe spoke to him in the calculus of the lower-brain language.

"You are counterprinciple," he said, "and cannot endure."

Satan—the structure—roared and came tumbling in great chunks down on Rafe. A hand seized Rafe's arm to pull him back out of the way, and he woke to find his arm being shaken by a man he did not know.

"Get up," the man said. "They're waiting for you now."

"Who's waiting?" Rafe asked. But the other stood back, folded his arms and did not answer. He carried a small green box like the one their original guide had carried and Gaby had taken apart, and as Rafe stood up he felt the broadcast he had first encountered on the aircraft take control of his upper mind.

"This way," said the man.

He led the way out of the rooms. They were joined by a man holding another green box who was conducting Gaby in her vehicle, and all four of them walked for some distance through a brilliantly lit, high-ceilinged corridor, until they came to a large circular room with one enormous window piercing the rock wall to look on sheer cliffs all around.

Beside the window was a low dais, on which were several men. In the center, cross-legged on a sort of backless chair, sat three plump-faced men in white dhotis, clean shaven, middle-aged, and with a serenity of countenance that signaled years of self-examination and self-training. To their left, away from the window, stood a tall, heavy man of about fifty, wearing a business suit with puffed shoulders and a blue-striped waistcoat.

On the other side of the dhoti-clad men stood two familiar figures. One was Peer Wallace, the crewman on the Project shuttle that had brought Rafe to Earth. The other was Martin Pu-Li himself.

Martin looked bleakly at Rafe, as Rafe and Gaby were brought less than a dozen feet from the edge of the dais. There was a chair standing empty there and Gaby was assisted out of the vehicle into it, and the vehicle taken away out of sight, someplace behind them. Side by side, she sitting and Rafe standing, they faced the dhoti-clad men.

"If you think I'm at all happy to see you here like this," said Martin bleakly to Rafe, "think again. I'm not."

The central dhoti-clad man raised a square brown hand, calmly.

"Let us put aside emotions," he said gently. "For it's necessary now that we all arrive at the truth."

9

"Why'd you have to do it, Rafe?" asked Martin Pu-Li. "You were perfectly all right, out of it, up on the Moon in the Project. Why did you have to go get yourself involved?"

Looking at the taller man, Rafe felt for a moment the old, gut-twisting sensation of sympathy.

"I told you before I put you in the locker in the gym," Rafe said gently. "You can't shut up people like me and expect them to do nothing."

"Was that it?" asked the central dhoti-clad man, and Rafe turned back to see that individual looking keenly at him. "Was that the only reason you came back down to Earth, because you were hungry for something to do?"

"No," said Rafe. "Things were wrong. The Project was at a standstill; it had been for three years. But Earth was still pumping trillions of dollars a year into it. Why? If there hadn't been something wrong down here, how could that much cost and effort go on without someone questioning the needless expense of it? But there was never any question—for good reason."

He looked back at Martin.

"Three men were running the world to suit themselves," he said. "Martin, Pao, and Forebringer."

"No," said the central dhoti-clad one. "Only one man runs this world."

Once more Rafe turned his eyes from Martin to the speaker.

"Who, then?" he asked.

The dhoti-clad man did not physically shiver, but something about him gave the impression of shivering.

"Shaitan," he answered.

"Your friend," broke in Martin harshly. "Abner Leesing."

"Oh, no!" said Gaby, in a tone of utter disbelief.

81

"Some of us are inclined to agree with you, Miss Leesing," said the dhoti-clad man. "Or, at least, we're still unconvinced."

"I'm not," said the tall, heavy, middle-aged man in the business suit. His voice was hoarse and abrupt. "Leesing's the one. And these two know it. Make them talk."

The coarse edge to his voice was like the rough surface of a file, brushing all of Rafe's nerves up on edge. He looked across at the heavy man and their eyes met. But there was nothing there behind the eyes of the other—no reason, no understanding; only self-concern.

"Something scare you, friend?" asked Rafe softly.

"Yes, something scares me," said the other flatly. He looked to the central dhoti-clad man. "We're taking a chance every minute we hold them here. So why hold them and not do anything?"

The man he looked at held up a square brown hand.

"We're going through the motions of passing them on right now," he answered. "There's a five-place ship waiting at the entrance. Meanwhile, we've got a few minutes, perhaps half an hour. Not enough time to force information from people like this, but maybe enough time to convince them to trust us. Mr. Harald, have you any idea who we are?"

"I think so," said Rafe. "You're all part of the organization, whatever it is, that runs this world now that it's half dead and dying a little faster each day. You're part of an organization, but even part of it you don't understand it much better than I do. Evidently you don't even know who runs it."

"The Old Man runs it," said the central dhoti-clad man.

"No," said Martin Pu-Li. "He's a figment of the imagination, a scarecrow—this Old Man of the Mountain, this Shaitan. Rafe, listen to me—"

Rafe turned to him.

"I won't say you're completely wrong in what you've thought," Martin said with difficulty, like someone pronouncing a death sentence against his own convictions. "Accident, just the accident of Pao, Bill Forebringer and myself being thrown together the way we were, put us in a position of responsibility we'd never planned on having. We almost did rule the world—maybe we could have. But someone—or some group—has beaten us to it."

"And the daytime's all you've got left," said Rafe.

"We did our best," Martin said. "We tried to organize the night people, the ones who could resist the power broadcasts. We had them going for a while."

"You took in anyone you could get," said Rafe. He was looking again at the heavy-bodied man, who stirred angrily.

"You looking for trouble?" he said to Rafe.

"Just remembering," said Rafe. "I saw your picture in the news a few times. You were an underground broker for East-West opium shipments, weren't you?"

"Take a leap," said the heavy-bodied man. "Take a flying leap."

"And that's how you got into trouble," Rafe said, turning back to Martin. "You took anybody you could get, anybody who could be useful—the underworld characters who could control the criminal element among the zombies, the people who were resistant on their own, the students of yoga and other sciences who had some control over their brain-wave patterning. And because you took anybody and everybody, part of your organization's got away from you. Hasn't it?"

"You don't understand," said Martin.

"That's right, Mr. Harald," said the central dhoti-wearer. "It wasn't a case of rebellious underlings getting out of control that afflicted the organization of the night. It was the discovery that from the beginning there was someone higher up than all of us, pulling strings."

"Leesing," said Martin Pu-Li.

"Someone—" said the dhoti-clad man, who had not yet taken his eyes off Rafe, "someone controls us all. Someone or something. He or it is master of the world, Mr. Harald—the real master. He can even operate by day if he has to, in spite of Mr. Pu-Li and Willet Forebringer and Pao Gallot."

"At least," said Rafe, who had been watching him closely as he talked, "whoever it is has made believers of you all."

"He'll make one of you, too, Mr. Harald—shortly."

Rafe shook his head.

"No," he said, smiling a little, "I've been self-trained too long. The concept of a better man than myself doesn't exist in my universe."

The dhoti-clad speaker looked at him for another long moment before changing his gaze to Martin.

"Is this what we've risked ourselves for here?" he asked Martin. "An egocentric? Does he really think he's that capable?"

Martin nodded.

"He does. He is," Martin answered a little thickly. "If there's a better brain in a better body, ten years of searching by the Project wasn't able to find it. He was to be our commander on the first ship out."

"Still . . ." the other turned back to Rafe. "We'll give you the benefit of the doubt, Mr. Harald. You say a concept like that isn't in your universe. A Shaitan concept wasn't in ours, either. People like myself, who've gone seeking an inner wisdom, weren't designed or trained to fight a war. Events pushed us into this—the nighttime broadcasts that left us among the only people capable of staying awake in a sleeping world. We faced what was."

"And now you're ready to accept the idea of an Old Man of the Mountain?" asked Rafe. "You're ready to believe in someone with supernatural powers and authority?"

"Not supernatural." The dhoti-clad man's voice was gently instructive. "No powers are supernatural once they're understood, and we understand such powers better than most."

"Do you understand how they could be used for personal, selfish ends?"

"No." The other stared with brilliant brown eyes at Rafe. "That we don't understand. Do you?"

"I understand how a negative mind could grow wiser and stronger—given enough time," said Rafe. Almost involuntarily, there drifted back across the stage of his mind the dream image of the underground caverns filled with empty and discarded things, where the enormous papery slug, or burnt-out fire pile, laired.

There was a faint sound that was not really a sound. Something like a mental *ping*, as the image formed in Rafe's mind. Abruptly, the room darkened slightly—not as if the light were less, but as if there had been a certain thickening of the air that impeded the light's passage.

At the same moment, the compulsion of the same broadcast power that had tranquilized him on the flight to this place flowed once more around Rafe. He made the mental effort to slip out of its grasp, and looked around him. Suddenly it had become hard to see—as if the air, in addition to having thickened, had become rippled and distorted. Up at one end of the room, the three dhoti-clad men had not moved or changed expression, but every other person in the room was caught in mid-movement to some new location.

The three dhoti-men were like Buddhas carved in light-brown wood. The tranquilizing effect scaled up in strength, then broke, disappeared. The heavy-bodied man stood with mouth open, jaw dropped. He began to yammer.

"The-bom-om-om. . . ." The sound went on and on and on as if he had no control over his own voice. "Shankar-ar-ar . . ."

There was a flicker of blackness among them—the cut-out figures, moving silhouettes of two-dimensional men, swinging clubs. Rafe spun about and pulled Gaby to her feet from the chair. He glanced about, but in the flickering blackness her vehicle was no place to be seen. He turned her toward the door. She stumbled, but managed to walk with surprising speed, his arm supporting her. On their way out, they passed Martin Pu-Li, pursued by a black figure that a second before had been invisible, edge on.

Rafe leaped in the air and lashed out with his right foot at the figure. It crumpled and disappeared. Rafe seized a dazed Martin by the elbow and shoved him at a run from the room.

Gaby swerved suddenly to avoid a half-seen, fluttering black shape, and once more Rafe kicked out and cleared the way. He felt the jar of impact up his leg, and then the corridor before them was clear. Together, clumsily, they ran.

They passed three more of the black silhouettes, but these were engaged in clubbing or knifing other inhabitants of this mountain stronghold. The air remained rippled and unnatural—thick and difficult to breathe. The three of them continued until they came at last to the open area just inside the slot in the cliff face where the craft that had brought them had entered.

The vertical door to the huge slot was raised now. On the floor of the open area were several planes of the type that had brought them here, and also a half-dozen trans-parent-sided, coffin-narrow craft within which could be seen the ranked bodies of men apparently in a trance.

They did not move except to twitch or change expression as Rafe and the others ran past, but from the open doorways of each of these different craft could be heard a heavy, grunting breathing like that of people caught asleep in a nightmare.

"A five-place ship, he said—" snapped Rafe breathlessly at Gaby and Martin. "Must be that one—over there —go!"

He pushed them ahead of him as two black silhouettes with knives flickered toward them. Rafe meant to meet them, being sure to take the nearer one first, and alone. He broke the figure's wrist, tripped the body—and found the second one on him before he was quite ready. He chopped out with his free hand, saw the second silhouette crumple, and turned, starting back toward the five-place craft.

Almost there, his knees went oddly weak. He was aware of Martin scrambling out of the craft to catch him, and then the light darkened badly. . . .

He woke to the steady humming of the plane. There was a constriction about his chest and he looked down to see his shirt off and a tight band of white cloth swathing him just below the nipples. For a moment he felt nothing else, and then he became aware of a deep ache in his right side, about the area of his floating ribs.

The face of Gaby loomed above him.

"Lie still," she said. "You had a knife sticking in you when you tried to get into the plane."

A wave of chagrin that was almost shame passed through him.

"I took too long with the first one," he said. "I knew I took too long. Where's Martin?"

"Up with the controls. Lie still!" she said. "There's no telling how badly you're hurt. Martin'll get us to a doctor."

"No." He shook his head. "Wait. Let me try something. . . ."

He closed his eyes and tried for the calculus of undermind thought again. It would not come. It was there, all right, but the excitement of other happenings since had buried it. He persisted, and then, suddenly he had it.

If the body is hurt, he thought, I ought to be able to feel exactly how and where. His different thinking roamed the switchboards of his nerves, not seeing but feeling.

"It's all right," he said to Gaby, opening his eyes. "No

real damage done. No bones, muscles, or major blood vessels hurt. Wonder why I folded up like that?"

"Lots of people," said Gaby angrily, "wouldn't think it was funny if they folded up with a knife sticking in them!"

Then she heard her own words and started to laugh. It was a sort of choked laugh to begin with—a laugh that was close to a sob—but it went on and grew into pure, hysterical merriment. She went on as if she could not stop and finally put her head helplessly down against the unwounded side of his chest. He could feel her laughing all through him.

Martin's face loomed above her head, looking anxious. "What is it?" he asked. "What's happened?"

Gaby straightened up and finally controlled herself, putting her hair back with one hand. She sobered.

"It's all right," she said. "He's all right. I just exploded, that's all."

"No doctor," said Rafe, looking past her into Martin's face. "Give me a hand up to the controls."

"You can't move!" said Martin.

"Can, and will." Rafe pushed himself up into sitting -position.

"Look out! You'll start bleeding—"

"No," said Rafe. "And I'm going to heal up faster than anybody in the medical records, too. Help me to the controls, Martin—or do I have to crawl there on my hands and knees?"

Martin's lips parted and closed. He took hold of Rafe's arm on the unwounded side of his body and helped him to his feet. Supporting Rafe, Martin steered him into one of the pair of seats facing the controls in the front of the craft.

"Thanks," said Rafe. He ran his eyes over the banks of instruments. "Good. You didn't wipe it off—"

His left hand caught Martin's right hand as Martin's hand closed on the controls of the autopilot.

"Careful," Rafe said. "I may be injured a bit but I can still break your fingers, Martin. Let go now."

For a second, Martin did not move. Then his hand dropped from the autopilot.

"Thanks," said Rafe. He touched the replay button of the autopilot, coding for the destination previous to the one Martin had begun to program. The destination-point map already on the small autopilot screen disappeared, and in its place he saw a map of England with a dot perhaps fifty miles northeast of London. "So. That's where we were to be passed on to?"

"It's just a location—a general location. Specific control takes over the plane when it gets close," said Martin raggedly. "No one back there—I swear that no one back where we were—knew who's waiting at that spot. If we had, we probably wouldn't have been questioning you and Miss Leesing."

"Then"—Rafe looked up into the other man's face— "why were you going to send us there?"

"We didn't have a choice about it," said Martin. "I told you someone or something else has taken over down here on Earth."

"So?" Gaby spoke behind both of them. "Shaitan—Thebom Shankar or whoever he is—was supposed to be waiting for us there? Then why did he send those shadows to kill everybody?"

There was a shudder underlying her words, although she kept the tone light.

"I don't know!" said Martin. His long face twisted. "Maybe it wasn't him. I don't think he—if it is just one man—is at just that dot on the map. That'd be too easy. And I think they were sent to kill us because someone found out we were trying to pump information out of you before passing you on to him. But that's only my thinking. I don't know!"

"We'll go find out in a few days, as soon as I'm up to it," said Rafe.

He reached out and punched the autopilot for the general destination North America.

"Where are we going?" asked Gaby's voice.

"Back to join up and hide out with Lucas," Rafe answered, and the aircraft, obedient to its autopilot, began a slow quarter turn to put the afternoon sun behind it.

10

"Lucas?" called Rafe. "Lucas?" Reaching out with his undermind, he found the wolf, and the mind of Lucas led him to the Canadian north woods, where Lucas waited by a pine-fringed lake so lonely and untouched in appearance it looked as if it had hidden itself successfully even from Blackfoot, Cree, and nineteenth-century furtrappers. The five-place aircraft reached the lake and sank down into a little clearing on the hard earth by the shore, under the light of stars only—for the sun was down back here and the moon not yet risen. Rafe sagged wearily in his seat at the controls.

"Come on," said Gaby, helping him to his feet. "You can't sleep outside. Martin and I set up a bed for you in the back of the plane."

"Not necessary," said Rafe, but the words came out in a sigh of exhaustion, and he did not object further as Gaby helped him to the rear of the plane. "This isn't going to be anything. I don't even feel too bad now—just tired. And I think I can heal myself in a hurry. . . ."

He let himself be pushed into the makeshift bed in the back of the aircraft and covered with blankets that smelled faintly of the mothproofing of an airplane emergency stores' locker.

"All right," he said. "But I'll be up and around tomorrow morning before the rest of you are."

Only he was not.

He woke later to fever and pain and drifted off into hallucination. Once more, endlessly, he walked the caverns where the hollow and useless things lived and the papery monster ruled. Now and then he was other places as well—places out of his own personal memory of the real world. But both there and in the caves, everywhere his fever dreams took him, there were pain and struggle. He fought or fled endlessly, emerging from his hallucinations to rest a little while in reality, then returning to fight with shadows and flee again.

When he finally came back to the real world to stay, he felt like a hollow man. He was aware of his own mortality, like a ticking clock inside him which must run down someday, and the feebleness of his own muscles was like a special curse laid upon him.

Fury moved in him against his new helplessness. But then that emotion passed and he was conscious of a new feeling, one he had never felt before. It was almost as if he were glad to be weak, glad to put off the feeling of physical superiority with which he had been born and which had always directed the course of his life. *Maybe I could be human like everybody else after all,* he found himself thinking, *if I stayed like this.*

The thought pierced some ancient barrier in his mind. For the first time he could remember, he was conscious of how lonely he was, how lonely he had always been— isolated by his physical superiority and that powerful empathic talent that every so often wrenched him out of himself and plunged him without choice into the minds and emotions of others. These two gifts had forced him to be superhuman, to be almost a god, whether he wanted to or not. And near-godhood had brought the loneliness. Now, he realized, he would be glad to give up his speed of reflexes and near-telepathic empathy altogether, just to be an ordinary man among men. But how do you give up things that are built into you—parts of yourself? Only death could break down the wall the two talents had raised between him and other human beings. He was cursed with strength as other men were cursed with weakness, and only death could lift the curse. But he was not ready to die yet . . .

"How long?" he asked.

"Five days," Gaby answered.

He shook his head weakly.

"You've been healing fantastically, though," Gaby said. It was midafternoon of a pleasant Canadian summer day. A watery-smelling breeze blew from the lake into the open door of the aircraft, and Gaby, with Martin and Lucas, was seated along the open side of his makeshift sickbed.

Rafe laughed—thinly, for lack of energy.

"In body," he said.

"You're just feeling depressed because you're weak,"

Gaby said. Martin said nothing. Nor did Lucas, whose animal eyes were steady on Rafe.

Rafe shook his head a little.

"No," he said. "I've been chopped down to size. Old mortality. You know there was a time when I really believed I couldn't be killed? Did I say anything while I was out of my head?"

"You were fighting something a lot of the time," Gaby said. "You talked a lot about gods not suffering. 'Gods don't feel pain!' you said, and 'Gods don't die!'" She looked at him curiously, frowning a little.

"One day we'll all be gods," said Rafe. "All of us. Not yet. We're still men and women now. I resent it, but it's a fact. We're still only human. And I'm just a man. But give me a little time, after all, and maybe I can go back to being the best man there is."

She frowned and touched his forehead with her hand.

"You're cool to the touch," she said. "No fever. How do you feel?"

"I'm through being out of my head. Don't worry," he said. "I don't feel good, though. I feel punched in the stomach. I've been reminded of my humanness and its limitations. I'm only a man, but I've got to fight gods. We're all only human, but we've got to fight gods. That's the way it's always been; that's why we need new generations, coming on new and new all the time to replace those the gods chew up or conquer. Someday, when we're strong enough, we won't have to die so soon."

Martin cleared his throat and spoke for the first time.

"He's still a little out of his head, Gaby."

"No. You're only human, too," said Rafe. He looked into the wolf's mask. "Lucas understands."

Lucas said nothing, neither with his artificial voice nor with the back part of his mind by which he had talked silently to Rafe across distance.

"Lucas?" said Rafe then, with the underneath part of his mind.

"I'm here," said Lucas in the same silent language.

Rafe looked back at Gaby and Martin.

"I'm all right," he said. "It's just that now I believe in Thebom Shankar—the Old Man of the Mountain or whatever you want to call him. That's all. But he's not Ab Leesing, Martin."

"You can't be sure of that," said Martin.

"I'm sure enough for our purposes," said Rafe. He struggled up on one elbow. "Help me outside. I want to get into the sun and the air. There's a cocoon of sickness around me as long as I go on lying here."

With Martin bearing most of his weight, they managed to get Rafe outside and onto his feet. Gaby walked now as easily as if she had never been crippled. The feel of the cool, open breeze on his face and in his lungs was like a miracle. Outside the plane there was a small, almost smokeless, fire burning; beyond it were a couple of bedrolls made of the aircraft emergency blankets, with a canopy of other blankets on stakes above each of them.

"I'm hungry," Rafe said, smiling. He turned to Gaby, but Gaby looked dismayed.

"There's nothing but emergency foods," she said. "Hard bread and some canned water. I can make you coffee or tea."

He stared at her.

"Is that all you've been eating for five days?" he asked. "Just what emergency supplies there were on the plane?" Even as he asked it, he knew it was fact. Lost in fever he had not missed food until now. But if he was hungry, she and Martin must be starving. He glanced at Lucas, who had followed them out and was now sitting, yawning at him.

"What's the matter, Lucas?" he asked. "Couldn't you catch them a rabbit or a grouse?"

"There's no game close," said Lucas unexpectedly. "I wouldn't leave Gaby."

"Of course," said Rafe, angry with himself suddenly for not thinking. To hunt meant to travel in these woods. A wild timber wolf had to cover many miles daily in a continual search for enough game just to support himself.

"Lucas hasn't even had bread," said Gaby. "I offered him some. But he wouldn't eat it."

"I know," said Rafe. "I didn't think, that was all."

They settled him by the fire with blankets around him, and he sat there chewing on some of the hard bread and drinking hot black coffee that Gaby made him from powdered supplies. The bread was unimpressive, but the coffee was like new blood flowing into his veins. He looked across the fire to see Martin now rolled up in one of the sets of blankets. A faint snore came to his ears.

"Five days," Rafe said softly, as Gaby came and sat

down beside him with a cup of coffee in her hands. "That's a long time for someone like Martin to be missing. Has he been wanting to get out of here?"

"He hasn't said anything," she answered. "I taught him about doing his natural sleeping in the daytime to get away from the effects of the broadcast as much as possible. I think he's changed his mind about some things." She looked at Rafe curiously. "What made you change your mind—about Thebom Shankar?"

He smiled. He did not realize the smile was savage until he saw the reacting expression on her face. Then he stopped smiling.

"Recent hallucinations changed my mind," he said. "Whatever or whoever's behind everything that's going on, there have to be two things true about him. One, he's real, and two, his tools are pretty basic. Or else he wouldn't be able to reach through to me and stir me up the way this is doing."

She sat cross-legged, the coffee cup in one hand with her wrist resting on her right knee, her brown hair loose now and a little fallen forward around her face as she watched him.

"You don't stir up easily?"

He shook his head.

"No," he said. "And for good reason. I've been a winner all my life. Something like that gives you a good deal of mass in the self-confidence area, and a low center of gravity when it comes to being jarred by the unusual."

"Where *did* you come from?" she asked. He saw that her eyes were hazel, with little brownish lights in them. He had not noticed that before.

"Everywhere," he answered. "My father was an architect—Sven Harald—"

She frowned suddenly.

"Oh, yes," she said. "The man who designed the Insurance Gardens Complex in Tokyo."

"And others," Rafe said. "All over the world. He moved. My mother and I moved with him. I was in and out of schools all the time I was growing up. It's the sort of thing that can wreck a kid. But I thrived on it. These reflexes of mine."

"That's right," she murmured. "Ab said you were unbelievably fast at everything. But I thought it would show—I mean, I thought I'd *see* you moving faster than other people. But you don't seem to do that. The only thing that shows is that you win."

"That's right," he said. "That's the way it works."

"But you mean just that helped you break in at one school after another when you were young?"

"Just that," he told her. "If you stop to think of it, it's the one thing that helps at any age. Strength doesn't when you're growing up, because there are always older, bigger, and stronger people to handle. But if you're fast, you can run rings around and duck away from the older ones. As a matter of fact I was strong, too, for my age. But that didn't pay off until I was about three-quarters grown. In the early years it was just the reflexes—and the mind."

"You had a good mind?"

"Yes," he said, and smiled again. This time without savagery. "I taught myself to read when I was three. That's the way it was around my father's house. No matter how big a place we had at the time, there was never enough room for all the books. He was a fast reader himself—those were the days before they began to think of speed-reading as something everybody ought to be able to do—and until I was twelve I couldn't keep up with him. He got himself new books faster than I could read them."

"He's dead now?"

"He and my mother, yes. Plane crash."

"Oh, no! While you were still young?"

"While I was at the university."

"Do you look like your father?" she asked. "Or your mother?"

The question surprised him.

"I don't know—my father, I think people used to say," he answered. "To tell you the truth, I can't remember. Want me to try to dig out the old memories?"

She shook her hair back over her shoulders.

"It's not important." She looked at him obliquely, almost challengingly. "You can't *always* win."

"No," he said. "You saw me get knifed. If I get lazy or careless, or let myself get boxed in by too much to handle at any one instant, I can lose like anyone else. But if I stay alert—and most of all, keep looking ahead so that I never let the odds get too great against me—I shouldn't lose."

"But you say Thebom Shankar—or anyway, all this talk about the Old Man of the Mountain—is getting to you?"

"That's right," he said thoughtfully, and drank from the cooling coffee in his cup. "I picked up a new trick on the way to that place in the mountains. I think maybe I learned something about it from Lucas. It's a new way of thinking that makes it easier to throw off a broadcast effect—any broadcast effect. It and my dreams and hallucinations tie together, somehow. I don't know just how, but there's a connection there. I can feel it."

Gaby frowned. The summer sun was lost for a minute behind a fast-drifting cloud, and a brief darkness came to chill them as they sat by the fire.

"I don't follow you," she said.

"I mean—" He roused himself from some new thoughts that had attracted him. "All these strange things have to fit together because none of them were there before the broadcasts as far as we know. If they fit together, then there's some kind of purpose deliberately at work—and it could be we're up against someone who's also not in the habit of losing."

"Another winner like you?"

"Possibly worse," he said. "Maybe a group like me." He stared into the flickering flames of the small fire. "Though it's hard to believe. It's hard to believe"—his tone was thoughtful, his mind half elsewhere—"even in one more like me."

"Why?" asked the voice of Martin, and looking over, Rafe saw the other man lying still in the bedroll, eyes open and gazing at him.

"Because," said Rafe slowly, "there's a polarization here. Call my orientation positive—that is, I've spent most of my life helping to push the rest of the world along the way it was going when I came along. The Project and my own part in it, for example. If there were another like me around, with positive orientation, we'd know about him, because he'd be doing the same thing I've been doing. That means that if there's even one other as capable as I am in existence and the world doesn't know about him, then his orientation ought to be negative—counter to the normal drive of the race."

"You mean he'd be evil," said Gaby.

He glanced at her.

"Good and evil are tag words," he said. "But use them if you want. The point is, we're opposed. And something else if he exists. I never suspected anyone like him could be. Even now I'm having a hard time believing it. So the chances are he never suspected the existence of somebody like me, either, and he's having as hard a time believing in it now."

"Your being on the Project was common knowledge," said Martin.

"But was what I am actually common knowledge?" Rafe answered him. "Nobody knew that. Forgive me—but nobody knows it even now, not even you two. The only one who could really understand what I am would be someone like me."

Martin lay there for a long moment looking at him.

"The world," the Project Head said at last, "is full of men and women right now who're scared to death of the Old Man of the Mountain. No one's scared of you, Rafe. I'm sorry; I don't believe you're as good as you say you are."

"I believe," said Gaby, leaning forward, her eyes fixed on Rafe. "I believe you."

"Think what you're saying," Martin said to her. "You're agreeing with him that your brother couldn't be Thebom Shankar because he knew your brother and knows your brother was inferior to him."

"That could be," said Gaby. But for a second her voice was uncertain. Then it firmed again. "No, I believe in Rafe. I know there's evil in the world. If Thebom Shankar is the center point for it, then there has to be a center point of good opposing that. And Rafe's the only person I've seen who could be that."

Martin looked at her with an expression somewhere between dismay and alarm.

"You keep talking about good and evil," he said. "You're drifting right back into the superstitious part of it. Nothing's ever going to convince me there's anything supernatural bound up in any of this." He turned to Rafe. "Rafe, you don't think anything like that?"

"No. Not in simple terms," said Rafe. "But you know, historically, there's always been a war between the two major impulses of man—to go with his society and fellow man, or to go against it and go his own way. You could call the first good and the second evil if you like."

"There," said Martin to Gaby, in a tone of relief. "You heard him. 'Good' and 'evil' are just convenience words to use in thinking about this business."

"I didn't say that," said Rafe. Martin looked sharply back at him.

"We may be up against something that hasn't been possible to us before because we hadn't reached the necessary technological level," said Rafe. "Our technology may just now, finally, have built a stage where the impulses of pure good and pure evil can fight it out."

"But there's no such thing!" Martin heaved himself up out of the blankets onto his feet. "No human being's either pure good or pure evil—"

"There are human beings who're willing to play the parts," said Rafe. "There've always been some people willing to try being saints or grand masters. There's always been another group ready to try witchcraft or Satanism."

"Sick, crippled people, with no real effect on the world around them. The people who played at Satanism and evil, I mean," said Martin.

"Did you ever hear of Aleister Crowley, the so-called Great Beast?" put in Gaby unexpectedly.

Martin frowned.

"Crowley . . . oh, the man around the beginning of the twentieth century who crucified toads and called himself 'The Wickedest Man in the World'?" he said. "He died broke and a drug addict, didn't he?"

"But while he lived, he did affect a number of people in the world immediately around him," Gaby said. "And he wasn't unique. I remember Ab said once, 'There's always a Crowley in the world, somewhere.'"

"Did he?" Rafe asked. "When?"

"When?" She looked puzzled. "I don't remember exactly. Some months ago. I don't remember how the subject came up. We were in the lab, though. . . . Wait!"

Her face paled suddenly. She turned to Rafe, almost appealingly.

"He'd just had a phone call—I don't know whom from. You remember my telling you how he admitted talking to the Old Man on the phone one night? You don't think—"

"When? When did your brother say he'd talked to Shankar?" broke in Martin sharply.

"He didn't say Shankar, he just agreed when Gaby kidded him about talking to the Old Man," Rafe answered.

"Don't let your imagination carry you away, Martin. Gaby, don't worry. Whatever we're up against, it's a lot bigger than a Crowley."

"But why would Ab say something like that?"

"We'll have to find out. And we will. Meanwhile don't worry about it."

"Meanwhile?" Martin echoed.

"For the next couple of days, at least," said Rafe. He looked back at the aircraft. "In a couple of days I ought to be ready to move. Then we'll drop you off wherever you want to be dropped, Martin. But Gaby and I, and Lucas, will be getting on to that destination near London we were supposed to be sent to. I'm eager to find out just who's waiting for us there."

11

Martin shook his head.

"No," he said. "I want to go with you."

It was three days later, and their aircraft was droning southeastward at fifty feet of altitude above the tops of the scalloped gray waves of the North Atlantic, Rafe having flown the craft as far northward as the Arctic Circle to avoid the regular aircraft routes and come almost down to sea level to get under radar observation. The sun was just setting, and they were less than twenty minutes from the Hebrides and the North Channel to the Irish Sea.

"It won't do you any good," Gaby said. "The broadcast'll be on and it'll put you out. Whatever we run into there, you'll sleep through it. Unless they catch us again —and then you'll get caught, too, without a chance to do anything to help yourself."

"No," Martin repeated. "I'm staying with you. I want to settle this thing now, one way or another—no matter what happens."

"All right, then," said Rafe, from the controls.

"Besides"—Martin smiled a little—"I might just be useful. I'm still head of the Project—what you yourself called one of the three men who run the world, Rafe."

"They were ready to kill you along with everyone else, back in that mountain hideaway," Rafe said.

The slow-descending July sun of these northern latitudes was still an orange line on the horizon as they flew in at last over the west coast of England somewhere close above Blackpool. But Martin already sat slumped in his seat, his eyes closed, his head forward upon lax neck muscles. The power broadcast was on.

Once past the coastline, the interior of the country was almost lightless. If it had not been for the autopilot holding a constant altitude, now of six hundred feet, and for the green-lighted autopilot map on which a crawling red dot showed their position above an area thick with place names, Rafe and Gaby might have felt themselves back above the Canadian north woods at nightfall. To the west the sky was still reddishly light, but below them was only a dark obscurity.

Lucas growled.

Rafe and Gaby, sitting side by side now in the two pilot seats of the craft, turned about to look at Lucas. The wolf sat on the seat next to the unconscious Martin, and his long jaws were slightly parted. They could hear his breathing now, hoarsening on the exhale to near growls.

"What is it, Lucas?" Gaby asked.

"Ab," said Lucas.

"What about Ab? Are we near Ab now?"

"No. Far. Ab's angry," said the wolf. "Ab's worrying. About you, Gabrielle."

"About me—"

"Lucas!" Rafe broke in. "Does Ab know where we are? Where Gaby is?"

"No," growled Lucas. "He doesn't know. He knows you're not home any more. So he worries."

Gaby looked at Rafe, then back at the wolf.

"Lucas," she said. "You must know where Ab is. Can't you tell us?"

Lucas's half-breathed growls ceased. He licked his jaws with a long tongue, then lowered his head slowly, slowly, until his nose almost touched Gaby's bare forearm where it lay along the back of the seat as she sat turned to face him. A whine came from his throat, and he licked at Gaby's wrist, apologetically.

"No," he said.

"You don't know?" Gaby said. "You really don't *know?*"

Lucas whined again and his tongue licked at Gaby's wrist.

"Don't know," he said. "Ab's there for me—not there for you. No use. No use."

He shoved his nose under Gaby's hand.

"Never mind . . . never mind." She stroked the rough hair between his ears. "It's all right, Lucas. I just had to ask. But it's all right. Never mind now."

He licked at her hand again and slowly sat upright once

more on the seat. Gaby turned back to the instruments, and Rafe turned back with her. For a long moment as they flew on over darkness she said nothing. Then she spoke.

"Ab must not want me to know."

"That's possible," said Rafe.

She turned sharply to him.

"You think there's some other possibility?" Her voice challenged him.

"Remember I found my way back to Lucas in the woods?" Rafe asked. "I told you I discovered something new on the way to that place in the mountain. I found I could *feel* Lucas—with the back part of my mind. The only thing is, to me he felt as if he were right in front of me when he was actually hundreds or thousands of miles away. I asked Lucas if he could feel me the same way. He said he could. I asked him if he could feel Ab, and he said he could. I think he actually can feel Ab, but either Ab's everywhere at once to him, just like Lucas was to me, or else Lucas hasn't got what's needed in that artificial speech center Ab and you gave him, to describe Ab's location when he feels Ab."

She stared at him for a long moment. Then she turned about in the seat and reached back once more to stroke the wolf.

"Lucas," she said gently. "Lucas . . ."

Eyes on the instruments in front of him, Rafe heard even over the engine's humming the noise of the wolf's tongue rasping on Gaby's hand.

"We're almost there," Rafe said. "We'd better start getting ready."

"How far away are we now?" Gaby asked.

"A little under ten miles," said Rafe. "Actually, sixteen kilometers. I'm guessing that in a part of the world with this much air traffic, they wouldn't want to risk ground control from more than a minimum distance—but that minimum distance can't be much less than fifteen kilometers for safety purposes. Dressed and ready?"

"All but my outer clothes."

She scrambled back over the seat as Rafe locked the autopilot on a small village churchyard some six hundred meters ahead in the darkness below. A moment later, Gaby slid over the back of the pilot's seat beside him, wearing the black waterproof jacket and slacks of an immersion suit from the same emergency locker of the plane that had supplied hard bread and coffee and blankets back in the Canadian north woods. She handed him a similar suit.

"Dress," she said. "I'll watch the autopilot."

He struggled to pull the suit on over his other clothes. It was not only waterproof but dead black, which would be useful to them on the ground below. A slight jar announced that the craft had set itself down in the churchyard, and in the same second, a white light on the instrument panel gave the same information.

"Give me a hand with Martin," Rafe said.

Together they got the unconscious man into an immersion suit and out of the plane. They laid him on the grass, with a tall and somewhat leaning headstone between him and the night breeze, which was damp and cool on their hands and faces after the drier night of the Canadian summer. Rafe stepped back into the craft to set the autopilot for automatic flight, then stepped out again, closing the door behind him.

"All right," he said to Gaby and Lucas. "We've got half an hour to find some transportation."

It took them almost the full half hour to do it, and they were forced to break open some garage doors and jump the ignition wires of an ancient panel delivery truck —but they were waiting in the vehicle, by the churchyard, when the aircraft once more rose into the night sky and flew eastward at the four-hundred-meter altitude and the crawling, ten-kilometer-per-hour pace for which Rafe had set the autopilot.

Looking up was markedly different from looking down into unrelieved darkness. The black silhouette of the low-flying, slow-moving craft was plainly visible against the clear, star-filled sky in which a quarter moon was now beginning to show. Rafe drove, and Gaby kept her eyes on the craft while he concentrated on the road. Even at that they almost lost their flying quarry twice when its path altered abruptly and it flew away from the road below on which they were following, out across open fields.

The first time this happened Rafe quickly came upon an intersection that allowed him to change the truck's direction and follow. The second time he merely swung the wheel, tore through a fence that screamed with the protest of wire stretched and broken on the sides of the truck, and followed across a meadow area until he could break through a second fence to pick up a road again.

Finally, a little way before them, they saw the craft halt for a second and then descend vertically behind some trees fronting the narrow road they were now on. Rafe brought the panel truck to a halt.

"On foot from here," he said.

He and Gaby, with Lucas, left the truck pulled off the road, half in a ditch, and took to the field nearby, making a circle to come up behind the area where the plane had come down. The destination was obviously some large, old house, protected by trees and hedges and also enclosed a fair amount of open ground or lawn. From the back, the protective belt of trees was thicker, but the upper roofs of the house still loomed blackly above them. They came forward to the trees, and encountered a tall lilac hedge, which Rafe went forward to examine cautiously alone. After a second, he came back to Gaby and Lucas.

"Wire fencing," he said, "and there's no point in its being there unless it's both electrified and alarm-rigged. It's about ten feet high. Lucas, do you know how high that is?"

"Yes," said Lucas.

"If I stand just in front of the fence and bend over—like this"—he demonstrated, putting his hands on his knees to brace himself—"can you take one jump to my back and then get over the fence with a second jump?"

"Yes," said Lucas.

"All right. Then that's what we'll do. After you're inside the fence, Lucas, stay close to it—there may be booby traps of some kind farther in, but there ought to be a clear track just inside the fence for inspection purposes. Follow around the inside of the fence, or any wall or hedge you come to, until you get to the front gate of this place. Then wait until I come up to the gate and try to get in."

"But there may be someone there on guard!" said Gaby.

"That's what I'm counting on," said Rafe. "There has to be a guard on a place as important as this. I'll try to get him right up against the inside of the gate, or whatever it is. Then, Lucas—you take him out. Quickly, before he can make any noise. Don't move until I say your name—then take him. You understand?"

"Understand," said Lucas.

"Good. Now, let's get you inside."

They went up to the fence together. Rafe spread his legs and bent his shoulders, bracing himself firmly with his hands gripping his thighs just above his knees. The wire of the fence, glinting a little in the early moonlight, was less than a foot from his nose.

"All right, Lucas," He said. "Go ahead."

There was a faint breath, almost like a whine behind him, a rustle of grass that would be the wolf backing off, then a brief, rapid thud of running paws and a shock of impact on Rafe's back that almost sent him lurching forward into the fence and knocked the breath half out of him.

With straining muscles he caught himself from that lurch and staggered erect. He looked through the fence but could see only darkness beyond.

"Lucas?" he whispered cautiously.

A whine came back from the far side of the fence. A second later a dark, moving shape occulted what little light was to be seen beyond the lower part of the woven wire that Rafe faced.

"Fine! Good L—" The words stuck in Rafe's throat. He had been about to praise Lucas as he would a dog. But Gaby was right. Lucas was something more than a canine. He was too much of a person to be rewarded with a condescending word. "That's a good job, Lucas."

Once more, the whine.

"I'll go now," Rafe said, turning right. "Follow level with me along the inside of the fence as long as you can."

He moved off. It was a long hike through dimness, for the place was not small. He reached the road again and turned left, going down the belt of trees facing the highway, watching the faint sheen of wire fence between them out of the corner of his eyes. Sure enough, after a little distance, a high stone wall appeared, with stretched wire along its top, guarding even the trees from the outside world. Rafe followed the wall silently, until he saw it interrupted by what first appeared to be a vertical dark line, but which soon widened to take on the dimensions of a gate to a roadway entering the place.

Rafe slowed. As silently as possible, he moved over the rough grass at the foot of the wall to the near pillar of the entrance, and looked beyond it. As he had suspected, there was a gate, wrought-iron, designed as if for appearances only. He waited a few seconds longer, feeling the cool air on his face and hands, his heart beating. Then he stepped beyond the pillar and walked to the center of the entrance where the two wings of the gate joined together.

He pushed against the gate as casually as if in broad daylight, and found a bar lock securing its halves at the middle.

"Hold on! Stand still, there!" said a man's voice from inside the gate and to the left. A door opened in a wall of blackness that revealed itself in the escaping light from within to be a gatehouse. The silhouette of a tall, wide-shouldered figure came toward him, the silhouette of a machine pistol in the crook of its left arm.

Rafe stood motionless on his side of the gate, squarely in front of the bolt that secured its two wings together. The twisted, black, wrought-iron bars were wide enough for his arms to pass through.

"Don't move," said the figure, coming up to the other side of the gate with the machine pistol pointed through the bars at Rafe. "Put your hands up!"

Rafe raised his arms in the air.

"Now," said the guard, pausing against the inner side of the gate. "Who are you? And what are you doing here?"

"I belong to that plane that just landed behind you," said Rafe. "I've got something to tell whoever's in charge at this place. Take me in—"

"Oh, no!" The barrel of the machine pistol poked through the bars against Rafe's stomach. "If you come through here, it'll be feet first—"

"Lucas," said Rafe quietly.

"Lucas?" echoed the guard. "Who do you think is Lucas? I'm—"

He was rammed forward against the gate suddenly, and his head snapped back. He sagged, but Rafe, reaching through the bars, caught him—a dead weight now, with his head lolling backward unnaturally on his shoulders.

Breathing heavily with the effort, Rafe managed to hold the body upright, first with one arm then another, while he went through the guard's pockets. He found a wallet, some small personal items, but no key. He let the body drop and paused to think.

"Lucas," he said.

The shadowy form of Lucas appeared close to the bars on the other side.

"Yes," said Lucas.

Rafe pointed to where a thin, upright line of light showed the gatehouse door still ajar.

"Look around inside that building," Rafe said. "See if you can find anything that looks like a key."

Lucas turned and went. The brightness of the door widened, and Rafe saw the wolf slip inside. He waited, moving back a little so that the light escaping from the open door would not shine on him. It cut across the still figure of the guard inside, but he hoped that close to the ground as the body was, and some distance from the doorway, it would not be noticeable.

Lucas came back and shoved his muzzle through the bars. In his jaws was a steel ring with a single key on it.

"Thanks," said Rafe. He took the ring and felt around the inside of the gate for a keyhole. But his fingers found nothing. The inside surface was bare. He gave up.

"Lucas," he said in a low voice, "do you know what a keyhole looks like?" He held the key and pointed it toward the palm of his other hand, making a twisting motion.

"I can unlock things," Lucas answered. "Ab taught me."

Rafe passed the key back through the bars to the wolf.

"Take this back into the gatehouse, then," he said. "See if you can find a keyhole somewhere in there that this works in."

Lucas's teeth closed on the ring. He went.

Rafe waited. He heard a slight sound behind him and whirled. He found himself looking down into Gaby's face, whitened by the faint moonlight. Anger and self-reproach hit him at the same time. He had virtually forgotten about her in the tenseness of breaking into the place.

"Go back to the truck!" he whispered to her now. "Wait there!"

"No," she answered.

"I said—"

"I said *no*," she repeated. "There may be electronic

traps or burglar alarms ahead. You may be good at some things, but I'll bet I'm better at that sort of thing than you. Besides, I want to go with you and Lucas."

"No," he said.

"You can't stop me," she replied. "I'll come with you—"

She broke off, staring past him. Rafe turned back to the gate and saw it opening. Lucas was standing just inside it. Rafe ran hastily past him to the gatehouse door and shut it, closing off the betraying light. He turned about to find Lucas and Gaby together, facing him.

"It's your funeral," he whispered roughly to Gaby. "All right! Come on!"

He turned and led the way rapidly but quietly toward the house, in the shadows of some bushes lining one side of the driveway. When they came to the point where the bushes ended, they were less than fifty feet from a corner of the house and perhaps a hundred feet from its front doorway.

The house stood still and silent in the night. Strangely, there were no lights showing about it, neither on the grounds outside nor within. Almost any place of size and value nowadays was brilliantly lighted during the dark hours and had video cameras at work to record the presence of any zombie visitor—so that he could later be found and identified in daylight. But this house, this towering pile of construction, seemed utterly lightless, without protection or even the presence of waking inhabitants.

"Too easy," breathed Rafe—half to himself, half to Gaby. He turned to whisper to Lucas.

"Lucas, do you smell anyone? Hear anything? Is there any sign of anyone anywhere around?"

"No," said Lucas.

"Maybe we're just lucky," whispered Gaby.

"Can't be." Rafe shook his head. "The plane just landed here fifteen minutes ago. If they've checked, they've already found it empty and know there's something wrong. If they haven't checked, why haven't they? That guard on the gate wasn't there for no reason."

Gaby did not answer. Lucas was silent.

"All right," said Rafe. "It doesn't matter. I have to go in anyway. Gaby, will you wait here?"

"No," said Gaby, "and there's no way you can make me stay."

Rafe shrugged.

"Lucas," he said, "if Gaby tries to follow me, knock her off her feet."

"Lucas!" said Gaby. "You won't do any such thing! Do you hear me?"

"Yes," said Lucas. "But I will."

"Lucas!" She stared at the wolf. "But it's me—I'm telling you not to do it. Why would you listen to him?"

"It's dangerous in there," Lucas said. "I have to take care of you."

"Who said?"

"Ab said," answered the wolf, "I was to take care of you."

"He didn't mean—"

Rafe did not hear the last of her whispered argument. He was already running for the shadow at the front entrance of the house. He made it and leaned against the brick siding to catch his breath. He was shorter winded than he thought, and his legs were weak. The wound, which he had almost forgotten—he had really done an unusual job of healing by applying the new-found attention of the back of his mind to it—now pained him so deeply it made him catch his breath if he breathed more than shallowly.

But his wind returned. The pain faded. He went quickly up the front steps and found the door to the house not only unlocked but ajar. Pushing it just barely wide enough for him to enter, he slipped through.

He found himself in a high-ceilinged entry hall. There were doors in the paneled walls to right and left and at the end of the hall a wide stairway, curling upward into darkness, with a tall window halfway up through which the Moon now gave a little, faint light to the hall's interior. He was able to see better than he had thought he would. One of the doors to his right was partly opened, revealing only blackness beyond. He went to it, but did not touch it—

A faint creak from the front doorway behind him brought him about.

The door was wide open now, and framed in its entrance were the silhouettes of a figure in what looked like baggy coveralls, and a dog. They came toward him even as he recognized them for Gaby and Lucas.

"Did you actually think you could make him disobey

me?" Gaby whispered fiercely to Rafe as they came together.

"Sh-h . . . come on," he said. He led the way through the open doorway into the absolute darkness beyond. "Just a second, while I find a light—"

The door closed itself behind them. The darkness was absolute.

"Will you walk into my parlor?" crowed a voice.

It was a child's voice, high-pitched, triumphant, and full of laughter.

12

Lights blazed on all around them. The impact of a different and powerful broadcast force immobilized them. They stood blinded and blinking in the sudden glare, and the childish voice went on in their ears.

"Stay there," it said. "Doggie? Where's the doggie? You had him with you. Doggie, wherever you are, you come to me. Now! Do you hear me, doggie?"

Rafe began to get his eyes adjusted to the light. He looked down the thickly carpeted length of an overfurnished room, its walls crowded with paintings in ornate frames, its occasional tables loaded with lamps and bric-a-brac. Light poured over all these objects from lamps and fixtures in every corner and angle of the walls and ceiling. At the far end of the room was a huge, throne-like chair on a low platform, occupied by an oversize, rag-doll-like caricature of a swollen human body; between the huge shoulders of this caricature peeped forth—like the face of a customer above the cutout neck of a cardboard figure in an amusement park—the beaming features and small blond-haired head of a boy perhaps six or seven years old.

"You did, you *did* have a dog!" the child's lips insisted now. "Where'd he go? Why doesn't he come? He has to do what I say—just like you do. Don't you? Take one step forward, Simon says."

Involuntarily, Rafe felt his right leg swing forward, and he moved one more step into the room, Gaby in step beside him.

"There! Now, why doesn't the doggie come?" The boy's face scowled for a second, then broke into its sunny smile again as if smiling were imperative to it. "Never mind. I'll get him later. Come on now, both of you. Come right up to the edge of my platform."

Rafe and Gaby walked forward and stopped, now less

110

than a dozen feet from the smiling child-face—and suddenly with his old, familiar, empathic twisting of the guts that put him unexpectedly in the mind and body even of an enemy, Rafe realized that what they were looking at was not some young boy peering at them from between the shoulders of some great, grotesque dummy-figure, but that the figure was a living body and that the child-head was actually attached to it. Behind that child-head, on the paneled wall, was a large, upside-down crucifix with something other than the usual figure hanging on it. A furless, rat-size figure, now blackened and dried, but which had clearly once been some small and living animal . . .

Rafe looked back at the grotesque individual in the throne before him.

"You see?" it said through the bright lips of its clear young face. "You have to do what I say. Everyone does. That's why I live here all alone except for a man at the gate. I'll have to get myself another man now. Your doggie hurt him so bad he died. Where's the dog?"

"I don't know," said Rafe. His own voice, in this brilliantly illuminated, cluttered room, before this unnatural figure, sounded strange in his own ears.

"He has to come back to me," said the grotesque. "Everybody has to come to me when I call them. I called for you and you had to come to me, even though you thought you got away when I had to punish them there in the mountains for not sending you to me immediately. Now you're here, aren't you?"

Rafe did not answer.

"Don't be sulky," said the other. "I don't like it when they sulk. And if I don't like it, they don't like it either. Stand on one leg—Simon says!"

Involuntarily, Rafe found himself lifting his right foot and putting all his weight on the left. His under-mind was searching urgently for the means of slipping out from the control of the broadcast now holding him. It was like the broadcast he had felt in the mountain stronghold, like that of the power broadcasts themselves, but much more effective and encompassing than either. Still, if he had been able to handle the others, he should be able now . . .

"I could make you both stand like that until you died," said the creature—it was hard to think of it as a man in spite of its enormous body, as long as it kept talking in its fluting, little-child voice. The clear blue eyes focused on Rafe now. "You know that, don't you? Say you do."

"I do," said Rafe involuntarily.

"Oh, but you've got to say it better than that!" The child-face was scowling again. "You've got to say it as if you *knew* it was true. Because it is. Don't you know that?"

"Yes," said Rafe, once more involuntarily. His single supporting leg was beginning to feel the strain. Beside him, there was a small noise, and out of the corner of his eye he saw Gaby fall. The attention of the creature in the throne turned to her.

"Why did you do that?" he demanded. "Is there something wrong with your leg, so you can't stand on it? Tell me!"

The power broadcast suddenly stopped. They were free of compulsion.

"I've been a cripple for several years," Gaby's voice answered from the rug. "I just started walking again a few days ago."

She climbed slowly to her feet. Rafe was measuring the distance of less than twelve feet between himself and the creature on the throne. If he could just get to the other fast enough ...

"You would, would you?" said their captor suddenly, shifting his eyes back to Rafe. "You'd try to hurt me, would you? Don't you know you can't hurt me? Don't you know who I am?"

"No," said Rafe.

"Oh, yes, you do!" The child-face looked angry. "I'm the one you wanted to find because you think I've got your friend Ab Leesing. And I have, too. But I'm not going to give him back to you. I took him to make you come to me. Didn't you know that? No, you didn't. But I did. Can't you guess who I am, now?"

"You're trying to tell me," said Rafe, "that you're the one who controls all the zombies."

"I control the whole world! Because now it's *my* time. The time of the Great He. The time of the Old Man, who's older than the world is old. The time of Shaitan —because Shaitan is me."

The child-mouth opened in a perfect oval as if it would sing. Suddenly from it came a booming, bass, thoroughly adult and masculine voice.

"I AM SHAITAN! Kneel to me! *Kneel to me . . .*"

With the first word the broadcast had come on again, and Rafe and Gaby found themselves involuntarily forced to their knees.

Reasonlessly the compulsion cut off again, leaving Rafe and Gaby still on their knees but in control of their bodies once more. They got to their feet.

"But"—now it was the child-voice speaking again, from a mischievous child-face—"you mustn't think I rule by might alone. My power is love, the love of those who worship me. And you've both got to worship me, you know. You must love me and worship me—no, you stop that!"

The child-face of the self-named Shaitan was twisted with anger, staring at Rafe.

"Don't you think I know?" Shaitan cried, in a high, tantrum-toned voice. "I *know* when you're thinking bad things about me!"

"You're getting readings on the electrical activities of our brains, are you?" Rafe asked.

The child-face of Shaitan fell into a look of blankness—a blankness that might have been astonishment and might not have been. Then it tightened up and grew sly.

"You are clever—clever," Shaitan said. "Very clever, Mr. Rafael Harald. But just because I use my little toys doesn't mean I need them. I can do anything I want, all by myself. Because I've lived longer than the whole world, and I know more than anybody or anything."

"Why have the toys at all, then?" Rafe said. "If you don't need to control people with a power broadcast—"

"Oh, clever! Cle-ver, clever, Rafe Harald! Clever little man who thinks he knows so much, but doesn't understand. I use it because I *want* to use it. My reasons aren't for explaining to little human men like you. Little human men who've turned on some lights and tell themselves now there never was a darkness—that darkness was all superstition. Only there really was a darkness. Always there's been a darkness. And now, at last, now that my time's come, darkness has come out again, too, to claim the world of little men. I was going to use you, Rafe Harald, I really was—and that's why I called you all the way from the Moon to come to me here. But maybe it's no use. Maybe you're one of these little men who can't learn. Wait. One more chance for you, Rafe, because I went to this much effort with you already. You don't believe in Shaitan? Look at your girly woman, Rafe, and remember the power broadcast is off!"

Rafe turned to Gaby—and felt all his muscles tighten. She stood now like a child playing statues, her body unmoving, but with the tremors of a tension running all through her. Her face was fixed on the child-face of Shaitan, and the frozen expression on her face was one of unbelieving surprise, of horror and wonder mixed.

"Gaby . . ." crooned the creature on the throne.

Rafe turned in time to see the great flabby body stir, come upright, and lean forward. The child-head, cunning with malice, stared down into Gaby's face. "Gaby . . . you love me, don't you? You love and worship me, don't you? Kneel to me, Gaby . . ."

Slowly, without any change in her expression, Gaby's knees began to bend and her arms to rise. She sank floorward and lifted her hands to Shaitan, as if in longing. Rafe's hair prickled on the back of his neck. The room seemed to have darkened about them, except on the platform where Shaitan sat. The darkness was not as if the lighting had dimmed, but—as back in the mountain stronghold—as if the air had somehow become a thicker substance through which light struggled to pass. Somewhere there was a humming like the monotone self-amusement of someone insane and withdrawn from the world, rocking out his life on some white-painted bench of a barred room in an institution. A smell like burning feathers and burning flesh together filled Rafe's nostrils, and his body was as heavy as a piece of the Earth's core.

And there was no broadcast power that he could feel being fed into the room.

Unreasoning, animal fear woke in him, exploding into fury. He reached for the calculus of his under-mind to grapple with the situation—

A snarl, deadly and wolf-born, cut across the still-murmuring voice of Shaitan.

The voice stopped. Suddenly the light was back; the humming and the odor were gone. Gaby's arms hesitated and dropped to her sides. Still on her knees, she looked around her, bewildered. Shaitan was glaring about the room. He came back to glare at Rafe.

"What was it?" demanded Shaitan. "What noise was that?"

Rafe did not answer. Abruptly, before he could speak, it came to him that he had heard the snarl, not with his ears, but with his under-mind. And Shaitan had heard it, too. But evidently, not clearly as a snarl.

"What was what?" said Rafe.

"You know!" Shaitan's child-face twisted. "You know! *What was it?*"

"Tell me what you think you heard," Rafe said. "Then maybe I can tell you what it was. I thought you said there was nobody else here but the gateman and you?"

"No . . . body." Shaitan's vast bulk shrank back between the heavy arms of his throne, as if retreating into a shell of safety. "But if it was *him* . . ."

Slowly, the child-face tilted toward the light and shadows of the heavily beamed ceiling overhead.

"Was it your voice, Father?" The tones were thin, thinner and more babyish than Rafe had yet heard them. "Was it?"

Rafe reached down to help Gaby once more to her feet. In the throne, Shaitan sat staring at the ceiling, little head pulled down between hugely fat shoulders.

But there was only silence—to the ears and mind of Rafe, at least. And, plainly, to Shaitan also. Because after a full minute, the grotesque man shuddered, a convulsive shudder that quaked his whole enormous body. He lowered his eyes once more to fasten them on Rafe.

"You're a fool," he said. His voice was still the voice of a child, but now its tone and phrasing were completely adult. "You don't believe."

"That's right," said Rafe. "I only believe in what can be proved."

"Proved? What more proof do you need?" The piping child-voice had a hard edge. "You're here—here where I called you to come. I brought you here."

"No," said Rafe. "I think I found my own way to this place."

"*Found* your way?" Shaitan's lip twisted. "You heard my call and came. I laid a trail for you. If you'd been less than you are, you'd never have got this far. But you proved yourself good enough to come to me—to *me!* Only because I wanted it. And now that you're here, you've got to learn what you are—and what I am."

"I know what I am," Rafe said. "As for you, you're a freak—"

With the last word, he hurled himself onto the platform and at the figure in the throne, right arm stiffly outstretched, fingers rigid and aimed at the pyramidal neck joining the frail young head to the massive body.

A shock, like that of running full tilt into an immovable wall, knocked the breath from him. His finger tips had merely dimpled the neck of Shaitan. He found himself held by the middle, held by the seated man like a puppy in midair.

The hands of Shaitan were enormous. Together they wrapped completely about Rafe's waist, and the strength of them was almost enough to prevent his regaining the breath that had been knocked from him as his attack was checked.

"Fool, as I said—" began Shaitan. Then he bellowed in sudden, mighty, bass-voiced pain. His hands let go, and Rafe caught himself from a fall to the floor as Shaitan's massive left arm dropped nerveless to the throne arm below it. Rafe had chopped down with the edge of his own left hand at that arm—a blow that should have been enough to snap a two by four of seasoned wood.

Immediately, Rafe was around the side of the paralyzed arm, standing half behind the throne. He threw his right forearm around the neck of Shaitan and pulled it up hard under the boyish chin in a strangle hold.

"Fool . . ." wheezed Shaitan, once again. Where he was getting the air to speak even that word was a mystery. "Kill me and I'll live again. Hurt me, and I'll find you and hurt you back. Can't you understand? I'm Shaitan—*Shaitan!*"

"Never mind that," said Rafe grimly. "Tell me—"

"Nothing . . ." wheezed Shaitan. "I'll tell nothing. And you'll let me go. You will because you love me, Rafe. You love me . . . and you worship me. You love . . . worship . . . me . . ."

Rafe tightened the pressure of his forearm against the pillowlike neck with all his strength, but the half-strangled whisper went on.

The very universe seemed to be changing around Rafe. An ugly warmth of emotion was mounting within him. It ate away at his will like acid, leeching the strength from the arm with which he held Shaitan. What had begun as a strangle hold was becoming, against his will, a caress. A sickly affection for the gross creature he was touching was drawing him down into its depths . . .

From the back of his mind came the suddenly wakened, ancient negative that had always refused to let him yield or be conquered. It woke his recently acquired strength in his under-brain area. Without warning, the familiar, gut-wrenching, empathic response was in him, but this time as a tool. He saw himself, and he saw Shaitan, as if from the outside; and he saw the pit of submission in which the other was trying to trap him by making its very ugliness and unnaturalness attractive.

The body response of the empathic reaction was like a flood of clean detergent scouring away filth that had threatened to clog his innermost self. He brought his forearm up against the pulpy neck with a new strength, and for the first time, the whispering of Shaitan choked into silence.

"Now," said Rafe into the small, delicate, childlike ear before him. "I want answers. Where's Ab Leesing?"

He released some of the pressure on Shaitan's neck so that the other could answer. But the answer that came was gaspingly triumphant.

"Do you . . . think I'll tell . . ." wheezed Shaitan. "I told you . . . I can't be killed. Even if I could, you wouldn't kill me . . . it's not your way, is it? And do you think anything else can frighten me? I've felt everything, seen everything, in this world and beyond. Give up, Rafe, give in."

"One more chance," said Rafe grimly. "Where's Ab Leesing?"

"Kill me, then, if you think you can," said Shaitan. "I still won't die. My body will rot, but my soul will enter into your soul. Bit by bit, day by day, I'll grow inside you—until I take you over, until you become me. Shaitan will come back to life in *you,* or in any man or woman who kills him. That's why I won't ever die. Whoever kills me, accepts me into him—to live forever!"

"That's what you believe, is it?" Rafe laughed so harshly that he saw Gaby, standing now watching in front of the platform, turn strangely pale. Rafe raised his voice. "Lucas!"

"Lucas?" whispered Shaitan, above Rafe's tight-held forearm.

"Lucas!" Rafe shouted again, and the wolf came into

the room through the far, dark entrance, where the door still stood ajar.

He came slowly, one paw following the other, down the center of the room, his yellow eyes fixed on the platform where Rafe stood with Shaitan. Rafe released the pressure of his forearm and stepped back from the throne.

"This is Lucas," he said.

He backed off until he came to the edge of the platform, and when he felt emptiness below his left boot sole, he stepped down to stand at one side with Gaby. Lucas came forward, his eyes fixed on Shaitan, singing with little growls in his throat, head held low and tail level behind him.

"Lucas has been made immune to broadcast power— all broadcast power," said Rafe. "And he hasn't got a human mind that you can make love and worship you. If he kills you, will you go on living in him, and take him over to live forever?"

Lucas came slowly forward, step by step, singing his growls.

"Doggie . . ." whispered Shaitan, his child-eyes staring fascinatedly at the four-legged shape approaching. "Good, good doggie . . ."

"He's a wolf," said Rafe.

"Wolfie . . . Lucas. Good Lucas . . ."

Lucas reached the platform and put one forepaw, then another, up on its edge. He stood up on the edge, his eyes still steady on Shaitan. Shaitan's huge hands, like the massive, oversize white gloves of some circus clown, rose from the arms of the chair, and the fingers bent inward at the tips as if to catch something.

"He's faster than I am," Rafe said. "And all he needs is to reach you once with those jaws."

"Lucas . . . good, good Lucas. You love me, Lucas—"

"No," growled Lucas, chewing the words. "You would hurt my Gaby, and Ab has told me to kill whoever would try to do that."

13

"Stop him!" cried Shaitan suddenly, in a high, thin voice. Lucas had already crouched, ready to spring.

"No, Lucas! Wait—" It was Gaby's voice, crying out just as Rafe also spoke.

"That's right—hold it, Lucas!" Rafe said. "Guard him. Just guard him. But don't let him move."

Slowly Lucas came out of his crouch. He stepped back so that his forepaws dropped once more from the edge of the platform. But he stayed where he was at the platform's outer edge, his eyes still fixed on Shaitan. Shaitan's great hands dropped soggily, heavily, on the arms of his throne.

Lucas growled.

"No," said Shaitan. "No, Lucas. I'm not moving." He turned his small face to Rafe. "The—Lucas talks?"

"And understands," said Rafe.

"Understands? Oh, yes." For a moment the child-eyes were half hidden under their lids, then they opened innocently once more. "But how much?"

"Enough," said Rafe. "Now I'll start asking. Where's Ab Leesing?"

Shaitan's eyes closed.

"I don't know," he answered.

"You know," said Rafe. He looked at the closed eyelids and the child-face that could have been sleeping. "Let's not waste time. I'll tell you a few things first to save time. The business of the power broadcasts putting people to sleep was only a side effect to begin with. But in the last three years that side effect's come to be the most important thing about the broadcasts—no longer just a side effect but the most important effect. It's been worked with and developed and refined by everyone who's been hoping to conquer the world or run it to suit himself. And Ab's work could counteract that effect."

119

He paused, but Shaitan neither spoke nor opened his eyes.

"There must be half a dozen refinements of the power broadcast being used by different groups right now," Rafe went on. "Some probably work a good deal better than others. Your version here works better than the version they were using back in that mountain hangout. That's one reason you could send men to kill everyone there. You did say you were the one who sent the killers, didn't you?"

Shaitan said nothing.

"Lucas," said Rafe.

Lucas growled. Shaitan's eyes opened suddenly.

"Oh, yes," Shaitan said softly. "I was the one who sent them."

"Good. Now we're getting somewhere," said Rafe. *"Where did you get them?"*

Shaitan's face did not move. He continued to stare at Rafe without speaking.

"I'm waiting for the answer," said Rafe. "You haven't got anyone here but that gateman, you said. Where did those planeloads of men come from?"

"From . . ." Shaitan hesitated. "You wouldn't understand."

"I'll understand, all right," said Rafe.

"They come from an island . . . an island, that's all," Shaitan said. "I can summon them—I, who know things no one else knows. But what sort of men they are, or where that island is, even I don't know. I only know how to summon and send them—and they go. That was how I sent them to the house of the Leesings, when you were there with Gaby. That was how I sent them to punish my unfaithful servants in the mountains—"

He lifted one huge hand again.

"I give you my word—"

Lucas growled.

Shaitan's hand dropped. Rafe laughed.

"You're lying," Rafe said. "They're ordinary men, and wherever it is they come from, you know where that place is."

"Were they ordinary men when you fought them?" Shaitan asked, softly again.

"No," said Rafe. "But there'll be an explanation for that."

"Will there?" Shaitan sighed. "Rafe, you're brilliant—in all things but one. And that's the thing that'll destroy you in the end and leave Shaitan as the winner, the way he always wins, in the end. Do you know what that thing is?"

"Tell me," Rafe said.

"Your one failing"—the child voice was serious now—"you're determined not to believe in the supernatural. No, you won't believe in it, no matter what. But you're wrong, Rafe. I tell you truthfully, you're wrong. Because I'm truly Shaitan, and I know the true darkness. As I told you, little men had it rolled back recently, for a century or two. But now it's come again. It's come to stay. The real darkness—from dusk to dawn, as the world turns around on its axis. And in that darkness there are real things—things that little men like you won't ever control. Did you know that every night now, as each one in the world falls asleep, he or she goes to hell? The hell that's *my* kingdom?"

"I don't doubt it," said Rafe. "But there's nothing supernatural about your hell. It's a by-product of the damage done them by the forced sleep of the broadcasts. Of course, you and others may be helping their nightmares along, with newer versions of the broadcast technique."

Slowly, smiling cherubically, Shaitan shook his head.

"And the men I use to punish? The men who send their shadows ahead to kill or injure?" he asked. "Are they by-products, too?"

"The technique that turns them loose from their bodies may be," said Rafe. "As for the supernatural—you said you could summon those men whenever you wanted."

"As I can," said Shaitan.

"Why haven't you brought some here now, then?"

Shaitan looked down at Lucas.

"Your Lucas would be too fast, perhaps," he murmured.

"Or perhaps you can't always summon them when you want them?" Rafe said.

He was aware out of the corner of his eye of Gaby staring at him. But Shaitan smiled.

"If I want them," he said, "they come."

"Call them now, then," said Rafe. "And we'll hold Lucas in check."

"But would you?" Shaitan looked directly into Rafe's eyes.

"As long as they don't attack us," said Rafe. "You can send them away again once you've proved you can bring them here."

Shaitan frowned slightly.

"Why this?" he asked.

"Because I don't believe you," said Rafe. "I think you can summon all you want, but no one'll come."

"You"—the child-face went ugly—"doubt *me?*"

"I doubt you," said Rafe.

"You fool!" said Shaitan, and his voice had deepened into the bass note it had found once before. "Push me too far and I can forget to worry about this talking wolf of yours!"

"You don't want to prove it, then?" Rafe said.

"No proof's needed," said Shaitan. "When I speak, the darkness sends messengers. Are you so blind with your determination not to believe that you'd risk my calling them here now? Remember, I can call them not by ones or twos, but by dozens—even by hundreds. Whatever happened to me, you'd never escape!"

"I doubt there's that many dozens to be called, let alone hundreds," said Rafe. "But as I say, call them. Or admit you can't."

Shaitan's ugly expression melted once more into the cherubic child-smile of earlier.

"I'll oblige you," he said.

"Rafe—" Gaby began.

He put a hand on her arm.

"Easy," he said. "Lucas, keep watching." Rafe himself looked behind him, around the room. It was bright and empty. He turned back to the platform.

"Where are they?" he asked Shaitan. "Not started yet?"

The child-face continued to smile, but the smile was fixed.

"They're coming," said Shaitan.

Rafe looked once more behind him at the empty room and back to the creature on the throne.

"When?" Rafe asked. "In an hour? This evening? To-morrow, maybe, or a week from now?"

"COME!" roared Shaitan, in his full voice, staring out over the heads of Rafe and Gaby into the room beyond. "I order you—COME!"

Rafe looked, found the room still empty, and faced Shaitan once more. He said nothing, only looked. Slowly, the tension went out of Shaitan's huge body and his eyes lowered until they met with Rafe's. For a long second they stared at each other; then Shaitan's eyes lifted again —this time to stare at the ceiling beams overhead.

"Father," he whispered, "have I failed? What have I done?"

There was no answer, from the beams or from any other part of the room. Shaitan breathed out slowly and looked down at Rafe.

"I've been condemned," he said emotionlessly. "You think my failure just now proves you right in your skepticism. But you're wrong, and you'll find that out sometime, sometime soon. Only that's no concern of mine any more. You move into even greater hands than mine now, and nothing matters—only the fact I've been denied by my Father."

He stopped talking, as if waiting for Rafe to speak. But Rafe only waited.

"Ask me anything," Shaitan said. "I'll answer you now."

"Where's Ab Leesing?" said Rafe.

"On an island—the same island from which the men came who can send their shadows ahead of them to kill," said the innocent mouth above the gross body. "The aircraft you came here in is still out behind the house. Take it, and punch out the code word H...A...V...N on the autopilot. The plane will take you there." His eyes closed wearily. "But nothing will bring you back—nothing, and never."

"Where is this Havn?" Rafe asked.

Shaitan answered, still with closed eyelids.

"I don't know. I've never known."

"You know how to get there," said Gaby suddenly. "How could you know that and not know where it is?"

"I was told," said the unseeing face of Shaitan, "in case one day . . . I might try to go there."

"But you never did?" she demanded.

"I would have wanted to come back if I went," Shaitan said. "But from Havn nothing ever comes back as it was when it went. Nothing ever really leaves there, just as the men who send their shadows ahead never really leave there, in spite of their bodies being sent on missions. You two will never leave it either if you go—and you'll go.

I see that now. Perhaps that's why my Father turned his face from me."

"This Father of yours, is he there?" Rafe asked.

"There—or somewhere else. It doesn't matter. If you go to Havn, you'll meet him," Shaitan said. The blood was slowly draining from his young face. It was taking on a pale and sickly look, as if life were being sucked from him even while Rafe and Gaby watched.

"Who is he?" Rafe said. "Your Father?"

"Who knows?" Shaitan's voice was weakening. "The Devil, maybe. Maybe a god. Maybe the God of gods if there's a God powerful above all others. He's like nothing else. Different . . . from all things. By this shall ye know him . . . that to him nothing matters. There's nothing he needs, and he wants nothing. What he does, he does for no reason at all. Just as for no reason he let little men roll back the darkness, or acknowledge me as his son. And now again, for no reason, he's let the darkness return. For no reason he smiled on me. And now, for no reason again, he's turned his face away, so that someone like you could mock me and overcome me. . . ."

The last words were almost inaudible.

"Shaitan!" Rafe shouted the word, and for a moment the closed eyelids flickered open. "Is he from some other world? Is he some sort of nonhuman?"

Shaitan's eyes opened all the way. He chuckled faintly, then chuckled again. The chuckle grew to a full-throated laugh.

"From some other world?" he echoed in a strong voice. *"No!* No alien! He's a man from Earth like you and me—a man, a MAN!"

And he lolled on his throne, thunderously laughing from deep within his huge body.

"How can he be a man?" cried Gaby. "You said he was a god!" He did not answer her but continued to loll on his throne, laughing at the ceiling. *"What's so funny about it?"*

"Funny?" He choked back his laughter at last and looked down at her, at Rafe and Lucas. "The fun's in the joke. The joke that's my joke. And I'm Shaitan—Father or no Father, *I am Shaitan!* I told you I'd answer your questions—anything you wanted to ask. And I've answered."

Lucas snarled.

"Yes, wolfie." Shaitan looked down at him, child-mouth still stretched in humor. "Bloodthirsty wolfie, who doesn't know the difference between mere men and women, and Shaitan. Cruel wolfie, who'd just as soon tear the throat out of Shaitan as he would out of any other thing with a throat to tear. Deadly wolfie, without a soul to lose, or a conscience to listen to. You don't understand my joke either, do you, Lucas?"

Lucas snarled again. This time more softly. His head had sunk again between his shoulders, and he crouched slightly below the edge of the platform.

"No, you don't understand—any more than these two do. But I'm going to explain it to them." He fastened his eyes on Rafe. "You asked me what you wanted. Have I told you what you wanted to find out?"

"You answered," said Rafe grimly.

"Yes, I did, didn't I?" Shaitan chuckled again. "I told you what you asked for because you threatened to turn Lucas loose on me. You threatened to kill Shaitan, and in fear of his life, he told you everything, —Or did he?"

"What do you mean?" demanded Gaby. She had drawn close to Rafe and Lucas.

"One thing. One thing that I didn't tell you." Abruptly, unbelievably, Shaitan's huge bulk was upright, standing on his feet. Lucas's growling rose to a thunder in the room, and Shaitan towered over them all. Now that he stood on the platform, his face was nearly eight feet above theirs. "My name—one of my father's names, but I can use it, too. I didn't remind you about it?"

"What name's that?" said Rafe. In spite of himself he tensed, ready for any action from the giant form looming over him.

"The Father . . . the Father of Lies! LUCAS—" bellowed Shaitan suddenly. "Kill now—or I'll kill you!"

Both hands outstretched, he plunged down upon the wolf and Rafe and Gaby, all together. Rafe dodged, but one massive hand brushed him, spinning him aside so that his own outflung fingers missed their target.

The snarls of Lucas mounted the scale of continuous fury. Outside of his field of vision, somewhere, Gaby screamed. Dazedly furious with himself for being knocked aside so easily, Rafe caught his balance, turned back, and literally fell on top of the prone body of Shaitan, chopping the edge of his right hand downward with all his strength.

14

He felt the whiplash strike of his right hand jar against something that felt more like bone than flesh. As he lifted his arm to strike again, his head cleared and he saw that there was no need for a second blow.

Shaitan lay without movement, front down, huge shoulders pressing into the carpet, and his head turned on one side, eyes once more closed. The green carpeting under and near his neck was moist, darker than the surrounding material. Lucas stood above the tiny child-head, licking his own moist jaws. Gaby was climbing to her feet, a little unsteadily, one hand pressed against her forehead.

Rafe, clearheaded himself now, jumped to his feet and stepped to her. Her eyes looked at him uncertainly. She did not seem to know exactly who he might be, or where she was.

"Here," he said, gently lifting her hand from her forehead. "Let me see . . ."

The area she had been touching was still free of any bruise color, but when he probed it lightly with his fingertips, there was a softness, the beginning of a swelling. Instinctively she pulled back from his touch.

"He must have hit you with one of his hands, too," said Rafe.

"I . . . think so," Gaby said. Her eyes were clearing. She felt the damaged area on her forehead and turned away to a mirror to inspect it. Her hands went from her forehead to her hair, which she smoothed and pushed back. She turned around once more to Rafe.

"I don't really remember him hitting me," she said, and looked down at the massive, still figure. "But he must have, mustn't he?"

Rafe nodded. Thoughtfully, he squatted briefly to feel with his middle finger up under the right side of Shaitan's small jaw, beneath the folded-up fat of the lower neck. There was no pulse.

He stood up.

"Why?" asked Gaby. He turned to see her watching him. "What did he mean about the joke of it—about his being the Father of Lies?"

Rafe shook his head.

"He was half insane, anyway," he said. "Maybe he really believed he was something more than human and he'd live again—even if an animal like Lucas killed him."

He shook himself mentally.

"Let's go," he said.

She stared at him, her tanned, gentle face stiffened in shock, still.

"Go?" she said. "And just leave him like that?"

"Yes," Rafe said.

She looked from him to Lucas. Lucas whined and licked up at her face.

"You—" she said, "you're a lot alike. You and Lucas."

"You think so?" Rafe said emptily.

"Yes." She turned away. Her voice was dead. "All right. Let's go, then."

They went outside, around the house, and into the open meadow where the dark shape of the aircraft they had used before stood sculptured in utter blackness under the stars.

"You're going there, then?" Gaby asked, still in that same blind, empty voice, as she and Rafe settled themselves into the two pilot's seats of the craft, with Lucas behind them.

"There?"

"To Havn," said Gaby.

"Yes," said Rafe. "But alone with Lucas. Without you. We'll drop you off near London."

"No," she said. "You know I'm going, too."

"Look—" he began.

"No," she said positively. "Let's not fight about it. I'll make Lucas help me stay if I have to. But it's not just that. You said back there that there were all sorts of variations of the power broadcast being used to control people. Maybe you really can shrug off the effects of some of those. But you don't know what you'll run into at this Havn, and I do. Or at least I've got a better idea of what than you do."

Under Rafe's hands the aircraft leaped once more into the air. Once they were well on their way to a maximum operating altitude, he turned to her in the little light from the instrument panel before them.

"You have?" he said. "How would you be likely to know what kind of power broadcast could be operating at this Havn island?"

"I told you I worked with Ab," she answered. "There're definite upper and lower limits to the spectrum in which a broadcast like that can lie. There's a similarity—has to be—in the devices used to produce it. You didn't need me back there, but I'll bet you'll need me at this Havn place."

He sat watching the instruments. The craft was climbing with speed. Shortly it reached its best altitude range of forty to sixty thousand feet, and he leveled it off, punching HAVN on the autopilot control-panel.

The aircraft made a hundred-and-ten-degree turn and headed southwest.

"We're in this together," he said at last, almost to himself. "I suppose it might as well be all the way."

He turned from the autopilot—there was nothing more for him to do with the aircraft controls, in any case— and swung his pilot's seat half around on its gimbals to face her.

"All right," he said. "What do you expect we'll run into at Havn?"

"A sonar screen around the island, underwater," Gaby answered. "Radar above. A pulse-laser horizon sweep for anything trying to come in on the surface between sonar and radar."

"In other words," he said, "we can't get there without being seen."

"That's . . . right." She caught her lower lip in her teeth. He chuckled.

"And," he said, "after we get to the island—what're we likely to run into?"

"Probably a general variant on the sleep broadcast," she said eagerly. "Either strong enough to make us completely unconscious or—as on the plane when they took us to that place in the mountains—just strong enough to have a tranquilizing effect. You see, the more special and specific the effect you want from a power broadcast like that, the more power you have to put into your transmission. It isn't just a matter of setting for a certain frequency and that's all there is to it. You can't transmit at all without transmitting over the whole spectrum at once. All you can do is try to get most of your transmitted energy maximized in a certain area by overlaying your primary broadcast with a number—anywhere up to five thousand—of weak, secondary broadcasts that are tuned to cancel out everything but the area you want to affect. Do you follow me?"

"Not well enough," Rafe said.

"Look—" she said. "It's as if your first broadcast drew a line clear across a piece of paper. Then, you erased every part of the line but just that small area you wanted to affect. Now, the smaller you want that area to be, the more line you have to erase. Eventually the power needed to get a specific effect down fine enough becomes so close in amount to the power of the original broadcast that you're essentially doubling your power input in order to get a fraction of it out, and the cost becomes prohibitive even with Core Power Taps. That's why the world accepted the soporific effect in the beginning, along with the power broadcasts. In order to fine the broadcasts down to the point where you wouldn't put people to sleep, you had to be using up nearly all the power available for broadcast. There was nothing left over to send out. Of course, the technique of broadcasting's been refined during the last three years. That's why you and I've been running into people who can get more special effects from the broadcast. But there's a definite limit. That's why I say we won't run into more than a single variant."

"All right," he said. "What if they switch from one variant to another on us?"

"I don't think they will," she put in. "I mean, it isn't easy to switch around. Almost certainly they won't try to hit us with first one type of effect, then another, so that we have to keep adjusting to resist it. The power that would take would be inconceivable. Almost certainly, they'll just pick one type of effect and stick with it."

She smiled at him.

"So," she said, "if we can just get on the island somehow without being seen, we can probably go where we want—or at least you can, and Lucas won't be affected, anyway—"

"By the way," he interrupted, "why not? I've always wondered why Lucas is immune."

"He isn't really," she said. "But what Ab did, as long as he was practically rebuilding Lucas, was install a microminiaturized broadcasting unit right in Lucas's skull. It broadcasts a signal that doesn't affect anyone six inches away, but to Lucas's brain it outshouts anything beamed at him from the inside. Of course, if anyone knew exactly what part of the available spectrum Lucas's unit was set for, they could cancel it out with an outside broadcast. But nobody knows that—Ab didn't even tell me—and trying to find it without knowing would be like trying to hit the combination on the lock of a bank vault by luck."

He nodded.

"So you see," she said, "we've got Lucas, plus what I know about broadcast power—and you. Once we get on the island we ought to be able to find Ab with no trouble."

"No trouble," he said, a little ironically. She stared at him.

"Why, what sort of trouble do you think we'll run into?"

"A lot," he said. "Assuming we can get ashore without being spotted, it's still an island full of shadow-projecting thugs. Lucas is vulnerable to the proper sort of broadcast power beamed at him—"

"I told you no one knew—"

"Except Ab," he reminded her. "But Ab's supposed to be already on that island. Maybe he's told someone there just what'll knock out Lucas. In any case he knows as much about broadcast power as you do, and then some. He can probably tell just what sort of mistake you'd be likely to make about it."

"But Ab wouldn't—" She checked herself.

"Maybe he's changed," Rafe said. "Maybe he's been changed. Remember, he wasn't taken from your house. According to Lucas, he left under his own power, and maybe willingly."

"Lucas said Ab was sad to go—that he hated the men who came to get him!"

"But he went anyway," said Rafe.

"What makes you think anything could change Ab?" she demanded. "What could?"

"Remember," he said, "how Shaitan told you to love and worship him? You almost did."

He had turned his face to the stars beyond the windshield of the aircraft, so that his eyes would not be on her when he said that. There was a little moment of silence before she answered.

"He was hypnotic, that's all," she said in a tight voice. "That wouldn't work on Ab. He's a lot stronger-willed than I am."

"It almost worked on me," said Rafe, "when I was choking Shaitan there at the throne. Besides, it wasn't hypnosis he was using."

"It wasn't?" He turned to look at her again. She was staring at him.

"I know something about hypnosis," he said.

"But then . . . what was it?"

He felt a tightness inside himself.

"Black magic, maybe," he said.

"Black—" Her eyes, wide already, widened farther. "You don't mean that!"

"Yes," he said, "I do."

"But Shaitan himself said your weakness was you refused to believe in anything supernatural."

"He was wrong," Rafe said. "I'm ready to believe in anything that works."

"If it works on *you!*" Her voice was close to fury.

"No," he said. "If it works anywhere in the universe I can see, touch, feel, or smell." He looked at her for a second, but her face did not relax. "Shaitan wasn't what made me think there might be some truth in something like black magic. I'd come to that conclusion before I ever started down from the Project on the Moon. In fact, that conclusion was one of the things that brought me here."

"You came down"—the words seemed to catch on her own unwillingness to say them—"because you thought there was something supernatural about what was happening here on Earth?"

"Yes," he said. "But supernatural in a special sense. Open your mind to the possibility, Gaby. Just suppose there's actually an unreal element in the universe—only, our western civilization's tried to deny it, as part of the development of our physical technology."

"I'll suppose it if you like," Gaby said. "But that's all I'll do."

"All right," Rafe replied. "Next, remember something else. Our technological civilization assumes its own fund of knowledge is growing all the time, continually expanding into new areas of ignorance, building more and more complicated tools for discovering what's unknown. With that going on and supposing that somewhere there actually is an unreal area of the supernatural waiting to be discovered, doesn't it seem inevitable that sooner or later technology itself would build instruments that would bring us face to face with the unreal, whether we wanted to confront it or not?"

She was still watching him when he had finished saying this. After a second or two she spoke.

"How can you know about something like this?"

"I know there's physical and psychological harm being done," he said, "mass harm to the whole population of Earth, and I can't find any real instruments causing it. So I'm operating on the theory that the instruments are unreal. If they are, then it's going to take a different sort of battle to destroy them."

"If it's true—*if* it's true," she said, "what can you do? What could anyone do to destroy them?"

"You can break the point off a spear, or snap the string of a bow," he said, "and that makes them pretty harmless as weapons."

"I don't follow you." She was frowning.

"Destroy the focal point of any instrument's effectiveness," he said, "and the effectiveness is largely lost. That gives you time to handle the situation the instrument was causing."

"The focal point—" She stiffened. "We did that—with Shaitan."

He shook his head slowly.

"I don't think so," he said.

"You think there's some kind of focal point for something supernatural—"

"Unreal," he corrected her.

"Unreal, that hasn't been touched yet?" she said. "You think it's ahead of us—on Havn?"

"That's my hunch," he answered. "But it's a pretty strong hunch. From the moment I landed on Earth until now, I've come pretty much in a straight line for this island. I think Shaitan may have been closer to the truth than he realized when he said I'd been called—but to Havn, not to him."

"Called—" she began, and checked herself angrily, then went on. "I don't mean to keep sounding like a parrot every time you say something. But you don't mean *called?*"

"Maybe 'drawn' would be a better word," Rafe said.

"By what? Why?"

"Assuming there's an area of existence where unreal laws apply," he said, "those laws will still have to have some sort of structure—a physics of unreality. And part of that physics may deal with a balance of forces. If I'm a plus force in the unreal area, and somewhere on that island there's a negative force, then maybe it and I are being drawn into contact."

"But isn't that just another assumption?" Gaby demanded. "First you assume that you're plus and something else is minus; then you go and add on an assumption that just because of that, the two of you have to come together. Why? Even if you're right about this plus-negative business, why do you and whatever it is have to come into contact? And why now, instead of last week, last month, or two years ago?"

"It's all assumptions," he said. "But I'm doing the best with what I've got to work with. But to answer you—I've got to come into contact with the opposite pole now to restore the balance I broke by deliberately coming down to Earth. As long as I was still on the Moon, I was one pole of a situation in balance. The real and unaffected forces were concentrated around me, the unreal and affected around the other pole on Earth. When I came to Earth, too, I invaded the territory of my opposite force. I destroyed the balance. That balance has to be restored, either by my going back to the Moon—and it's probably too late for that now—or by a meeting between myself and my opposite force, in which one of us cancels the other out."

She sat looking at him. He looked back. After a little while, it became evident that neither one of them had more to say in that particular conversation.

"How are we going to get ashore on the island without being found out?" Gaby asked at last in hardly more than a whisper.

"I don't think we can," he said. "I'm not going to try.

You'd better rest if you can. We'll probably be there in a matter of a few hours, the way we're traveling now."

She glanced at the instrument panel. The aircraft had climbed gradually and was now at sixty thousand feet, traveling at fourteen hundred miles an hour, still in a southwesterly direction.

She nodded, curled up in her seat, and closed her eyes.

Rafe sat back in his own seat, letting his muscles go limp. But he did not close his eyes. Instead he stared out at the black firmament, with its pattern of stars that seemed to change only at the pace of a snail's crawl, as the five-place aircraft flung itself around the curve of the Earth at more than twice the speed of sound.

15

The earlier pattern of stars which Rafe had gazed at over the British Isles had given way to an equatorial one before the aircraft began automatically to descend. It came down into a night of Caribbean softness, onto a dark body of land the full extent of which could not be seen, and which seemed utterly lightless from the angle of their approach. They landed with a crackling of branches, followed by silence.

In her seat, in the little glow of light from the instrument panel, Gaby still slept. Rafe reached out, opened the door on his side of the aircraft, and stepped down onto what felt like sand. The dark shape of coniferlike trees surrounded him. He turned back to the open doorway of the craft to speak to Lucas.

"I'm going to look around," he said softly. "Stay with Gaby—"

But even as he spoke, Lucas was slipping out the open door and was abruptly lost in the darkness.

"Lucas!" Rafe called in a harsh whisper. "Lucas!"

He stood still, waiting. The branches of the surrounding trees creaked against one another in the warm, damp breeze moving through the night, but the wolf did not answer or return.

After a minute, Rafe closed the door of the plane and went quietly over the sand, and between the trees, toward a lighter patch of ground a little way off that looked like it might be an open space. He reached it a few seconds later and looked around him. To his right the tree shapes thinned out to give a faintly moonlit view of a stretch of beach, and now that he was a little away from the sounds the tree branches made in the wind, his ears were filled by the faintly hissing sounds of a gentle surf. They had come down near the edge of the island, in an apparently deserted part of it—and this, thought

Rafe, was odd. It would be reasonable to expect the autopilot to set the aircraft down at some regular landing area and close to whatever buildings there were on Havn.

Unless there had been necessary some specific correction of the autopilot, which Shaitan had either not known about or had deliberately not told him. Possibly the autopilot had been programmed to put them down in an area which deliberately labeled them as unauthorized intruders. Or perhaps the landing here was part of the supernatural, the unreal—

Swiftly, almost before the thought had fully formed in his mind, he spun about. He ran back through the trees to the place where he had left the aircraft.

It was gone.

Anger at himself boiled up in him. It would be no trick to make the aircraft disappear. It was quiet enough in operation to take off without being heard, while he stood listening to the sound of the surf. But what more simple-minded way to isolate unauthorized visitors than to have an incoming aircraft make a momentary, false landing in an out-of-the-way corner of the island, and wait until those within it stepped out, before lifting and flying on in to its actual destination? Visitors who knew what to expect would need only to stay aboard the craft until it took off again for the real landing spot.

Now, here he was, effectively separated from Gaby. And Lucas? It was still not clear what had made the wolf leave the craft and refuse to return when called.

Maybe, thought Rafe grimly, the secret of the power broadcast wavelength on which Lucas could be controlled was indeed known, and the wolf had been commanded to leave. It was unlikely anything else would have taken him away from Gaby. No one else could call Lucas and have him come regardless. Wait a minute, Rafe thought. Of course. There was one person. Ab himself. If Ab had called the wolf, Lucas would have gone without hesitation. There was the choice. A power broadcast or Ab. No other reason—

Rafe checked himself in mid-thought, with a feeling of self-disgust. He had forgotten the most obvious possible reason for Lucas's vanishing. Ab had told the wolf earlier to stay out of sight when strangers were around. Lucas could have smelled or heard something that sent him into hiding. In fact, this was the most sensible explanation for the wolf's actions. What, thought Rafe, was wrong with him—not to have realized this at once?

The night wind was suddenly cold on his damp face. Without hesitating, he turned and ran, half bent over to stay below the lower limbs of the trees. He ran blindly through the grove until breathlessness slowed him, and he stopped. Standing among the half-seen trees, with his heart pounding against his chest wall, he tried to take hold of the realization that had erupted in him as he stood where the aircraft had landed itself not many minutes before. It was ridiculous that he had not realized it from the moment he set foot on the sand of the island, but his very slowness in recognizing what was happening to him was proof of the happening itself.

Twice, now, he had worked his way to an obvious conclusion as clumsily and painfully as a mathematics illiterate counting on his fingers.

Something was paralyzing his mental processes, slowing him down to a fraction of his ordinary capabilities. Standing in the tropical night with the perspiration rolling down his face and soaking his shirt to his body, Rafe tried to sense what was affecting him.

But there seemed to be nothing. The palpable touch of a power broadcast upon his mind, with which he had become familiar, was not noticeable here. Even the obvious distortion of his emotions that Shaitan had attempted upon him was not perceptible. Rafe *felt* perfectly normal. It was only the recent, abstract evidence of the slowness of his reasoning processes that gave any clue of a change in him.

Alone, separated from Lucas and Gaby, and in unknown territory, with this crippling effect clogging his mind, what could he do?

Slowly, so slowly that he swore inwardly at himself, came the obvious answer.

He went to the calculus of his under-mind.

Abruptly he was free. He was like a man conscious only of being soaked, who dodges into the shelter of a building and only then, when he turns and looks out the window, notices that the thunderstorm's rain clouds are in passage and the sky is clearing behind them.

From his under-mind, he could look at his upper mental processes and see them slowed and clumsy, as if by the action of a heavy drug. It was another refinement of the power-broadcast side effects he was experiencing, nothing more, but a side effect that was its own reinforcement. On the other hand—Rafe smiled to himself a little—it had driven him to take refuge in his undermind, and his under-mind was possibly better suited than his upper mental centers to protect him now. That part of his control center was closer to the old feral instincts, and he thought instinctively, like the hunted animal that he would be shortly—if he was not already.

Reaching out with his under-mind now, he felt for Lucas the way he had felt for the wolf when he had been on the aircraft that had taken Gaby and himself as prisoners to the mountain stronghold. For a moment there was nothing, and then the feel of Lucas's presence came to him—but no indication of where the wolf might be in body.

"Lucas?" Rafe called with the back of his mind.

Lucas did not answer. Rafe waited, then called again. He called several times, but no response came. The feeling came strongly to him that the wolf was aware of being summoned, but that something else was occupying him with an importance that left him no time or energy to spare in answering Rafe.

Rafe put Lucas from his mind. Whatever was holding the attention of the wolf was enough to make him useless as a source of aid. Rafe was on his own. As he faced this fact, his under-mind came smoothly to grips with the situation, and he began to move—not running now, but walking swiftly and making an effort to study and memorize the terrain as he went.

One thing was clear. He would be sought for first around the area where the aircraft had originally landed. The more space he put between himself and that location, the more time and space he would pick up in which to plan and operate. He was traveling parallel to the beach, but only as a means of keeping his sense of direction. After about twelve minutes of this he saw what he had been looking for—a hill rising inland from the water's edge to some farther height of land. He turned his back to the surf and began to climb the slope.

It took him about ten minutes to reach the top of the hill. The summit was almost treeless, and from there he had a good view of the bulk of the island stretching away below him, dark in contrast to the more reflective surface of the surrounding ocean. He saw what he had climbed up there to find. Less than a mile away, the beach curved inward into a small bay or lagoon, with the faint, broken white line of surf barely visible across the narrow mouth of its opening to the sea. On the inner curve of that bay a sprinkling of fireflylike lights picked out the shape of what was either one large, many-level building or a close cluster of buildings.

At the same time he saw something else from the height of his point of observation—a brightening line along the eastern horizon that was the first sign of dawn. He turned back to look at the cluster of firefly lights in the lower darkness of the bay. The sea wind was on his right cheek, and he could use that to guide him—though it was unlikely, at such a short distance, that he could miss his way, even if he cut directly through the wild growth of the island instead of following the shore around to the buildings.

He made up his mind and plunged ahead down the farther slope of his hill on a direct line for the lights he had seen.

He went quickly, but this was the tropics and dawn came fast. Long before he got close enough to see the buildings beyond a strip of tailored lawn, through the wild conifers and some low, scrubby palms, it was all but full daylight.

When he halted at last, still hidden within a clump of the conifers, at the edge of the neatly mown grass, he saw that the buildings he had looked at were, indeed, all connected into one large establishment. No one was in sight, however. It was possible at this early hour that most of them were still sleeping.

He could see no sign of any aircraft from his present position. It would be sensible to make a circuit of the buildings, staying out of sight in the trees, until he found wherever planes were parked. There was just a chance that coming in during the small hours of the night as it had, their craft had not been noticed or examined yet, and Gaby might be free somewhere near it—or even still asleep on the seat as he had last seen her.

Rafe began to move through the trees and other cover fringing the lawns and buildings. The circuit he made was not a short one. Once he came across what seemed to be a half-size golf course and, rather than go around, he took the risk of crossing it in the open, though he kept close to the ground and made the crossing keeping whenever possible a rise of ground between himself and the buildings.

He came at last to the air park he had been hunting. It was a gray platform of concrete, perhaps half an acre in width, with twelve aircraft of varying middle sizes on it. Only one five-place plane was among these, and it was either the craft in which they had come to Havn or that craft's twin.

Rafe paused to catch his breath. He was wet with sweat again, in the rising temperature of day. Abruptly, the inhibiting broadcast effect that had driven him to his under-mind disappeared. He was suddenly clearheaded. Gratefully he moved back into his upper mind. There was a rustle of tree branches behind him, and he whirled about.

"Lucas—" he said, and broke off.

Facing him was not Lucas, but a large German shepherd, wearing the harness of a guard dog. It stood less than a dozen feet from him, its upper lip lifted above its teeth. As he faced it, it snarled softly, and came slowly forward, stiff step by stiff step, its eyes fixed on him.

Rafe stood with his legs together and his arms at his side. He did not move. If the dog was one with guard instinct and properly trained, it could be almost as deadly as Lucas to an unarmed man. Those half-parted jaws facing him now were capable of exerting three hundred pounds and more of pressure behind the gleaming teeth— enough to snap the bones of his forearm or slash the muscle of one of his legs and hamstring him. In its own way, the guard dog was as much a professional as Rafe himself. His only hope was that the animal would come within reach before its handler showed up. Then, if Rafe wanted to sacrifice a left arm, he would stand at least a fair chance of getting to some vulnerable spot on the dog with a hand edge or toe, as the dog's teeth locked in the arm.

But the animal's snarls had been rising in pitch, and while it was still a wary six feet or so from Rafe, a man carrying a machine pistol pushed through the trees behind it.

"What've you got, King?" the dog's handler said. "Somebody from the kitchen again? Oh, oh—stand still, friend."

"I am still," said Rafe.

"Seen dogs like this before, have you?" said the handler. "You're a wise man." He was short and broad, with a stubble of reddish hair on the back of an otherwise bald head. He snapped a leash to the harness of the guard dog and motioned with his machine pistol. "All right. We go that way—up to the place."

Rafe turned and walked off. The guard dog had fallen silent, but he could hear the sound of the handler's footsteps behind him on the grass. They crossed the lawn and went in through a doorway, down a small hall, and into what seemed to be a very large kitchen.

"Take a chair—there!" ordered the guard. Rafe sat down gratefully and heavily in the straight-backed chair at the metal table the handler had indicated. He had covered some distance, mainly over rough country and through loose sandy soil in the last couple of hours, and to sit down felt good.

"Knocked out?" said the handler unexpectedly. "Want some coffee and something to eat?"

Rafe nodded.

"I'd appreciate it," he said.

"We'll get you something. Stay where you are now. I'm going to call in about you. Hold, King!"

The dog, which had sat down on the clean tile floor of the kitchen, was abruptly on all four feet again, staring at Rafe. He did not snarl now, but he was obviously ready for action.

Rafe sat still. After a few minutes the handler came back with a cup of black coffee and a plate with some scrambled eggs, bacon, and toast on it. He put the cup and plate down with a knife and fork before Rafe.

"Help yourself," the man said. "Just don't try to get up from the chair or make any sudden move. King's watching."

"Don't worry," said Rafe.

He dug into the food. He was just finishing it when a big young man appeared, wearing yellow boots, a green shirt, and green slacks.

"Bring him along," the newcomer told the handler.

"Where?" asked the handler, getting up from the chair in which he had been sitting.

"The big room," said the other, turning and leading off.

"Come on," said the handler to Rafe.

Rafe rose. Trailed by the handler and King, he followed the yellow boots out of the kitchen, along a series of halls, and both up and down several escalator flights. They came at last to a hall wider than the ones they had passed through earlier. Its high, cream-marble walls were bare except for an occasional tapestry or large, heavy-framed painting.

They came at last to a wide-open pair of ornate metal doors reaching from the floor almost to the ceiling. Instead of leading Rafe through those doors, however, the young man in the yellow boots stopped and motioned Rafe through on his own.

"Go ahead," he said. "They're expecting you. Let him go on alone, Jafer."

Rafe paused a moment, then turned and went through the doors, hearing his boots sound alone on the stonelike floor, without the echo of other boots or dog's toenails clicking behind him.

As he stepped through the entrance he felt the light touch of some other version of the power broadcast. Automatically this time, he went to his under-mind without hesitation and without breaking step as he entered the room.

Within the long, lofty, ballroomlike chamber were perhaps a dozen people standing or sitting in a group near its far end, where there was a small group of armchairs and sofas clustered to one side below a platform. On the platform was a thronelike chair very similar to Shaitan's. They turned to look at Rafe as he came close, and he recognized almost half of them.

Pao Gallot was there. So was Willet Forebringer, stiffly upright in a massively overstuffed armchair. Standing almost beside Forebringer was a man named Elowa Ehouka, who was a member of Pao Gallot's Power Broadcast Control Board, and several other well-known Earth politicians. But what caught Rafe's attention and held it was the sight of Abner Leesing seated in one of the big armchairs, with Martin Pu-Li and Gaby standing beside him.

Rafe looked at these two, and they looked back as his

legs carried him down the length of the room until he stopped before them.

"Here you are," said Rafe.

"Yes. Isn't it wonderful?" Gaby smiled at him. "Martin was right, Rafe. Ab is the one who's in charge of everything, after all, and it's all wonderful—only people just don't realize it yet."

16

Rafe looked down at Ab, who smiled up at him, but stayed seated in the armchair. Here, side by side with his sister, he showed the family relationship. He was slim and long-boned, like Gaby, with brown eyes and brown hair that was beginning to recede from his temples. His mouth was cheerfully wide, and his gaze was frank and open.

"So you're the Old Man of the Mountain?" Rafe said.

"I'm afraid so," answered Ab. He did not get up from the chair, but continued to sit as if he belonged where he was. "Sorry we had to put you and Gaby through it like this, but we'd reached a tricky stage in managing things. My original idea was that Gaby would be safer not knowing what was going on, and then by the time you decided to mix in it, the fight was already on."

"The fight was with Shaitan, Rafe," Gaby said. "He was trying to take over control from Ab."

"That's right," said Ab. "I had—we had to work with him at first when the power broadcasts went on. He had influence over a good number of zombies who saw their chance to do what they wanted during the night hours when the broadcasts were on. But he was bright—dawn bright, Rafe. It was just a matter of time until he worked out the whole picture of what we were doing, and got himself in a position where he could try to knock us out and use the organization for himself."

"And what was it exactly you were doing?" Rafe asked.

Ab lifted a hand modestly and grinned.

"Trying to ride the tiger," he said. "You were right about what you told Gaby. I should've known someone like you, Rafe, would be halfway to figuring things out as soon as you had a couple of clues. As you told her, the side effects of the power broadcasts have turned out to be the important ones. They tap an area of—well, I suppose

144

you'd have to call it psychic power. Power we can use to move civilization forward a thousand years overnight. The only trouble's been that when we went to use it we ran into the old problem—people who saw it as something they could use for themselves. But we've got those people stopped now."

"That's good to hear," said Rafe. "Only, why didn't you trust Gaby or me from the beginning?"

As he spoke, he was carefully examining the room around him. Halfway up the walls on either side were great open windows, unglassed and unscreened, with the tips of some large Dieffenbachia leaves just showing over their sills. From other, unseen bushes or flowers below these man-high plants, there wafted into the room a perfume of blossoms or fruit. It was a little heavy in its sweetness, as if what produced it was overripe or past its bloom. The new power-broadcast effect Rafe had felt on entering this room was still exerting its pressure on his upper mind. His consciousness felt it, from down below in the safety of his under-mind. Why a power broadcast if Ab was now being completely frank?

"I'm sorry, Rafe," Ab was saying. "*I* trusted you. But I wasn't alone in this—I'm not now. We have to think as a group and that means not taking chances—even now. I did what I could by first trying to put you in protective custody in Duluth, with Bill Forebringer's help—" He looked across at the stiffly-sitting UN Marshal. "And when that didn't work, I sent Martin ahead to the mountain headquarters to help look out for both of you."

"Thanks," said Rafe dryly.

"I know," said Martin, wincing, "it turned out you were the one who had to look after me—as well as Gaby. Shaitan hit the place there faster than we thought. He must've already been suspecting Ab was ready to move, and he probably thought you were one of us—an instrument of Ab's, maybe—sent to get rid of him. Anyway, since Ab's apologized I ought to apologize, too, for treating you like someone who didn't deserve to know what was going on—when it was you who sent Ab to me in the first place. But we had to think of protecting our whole effort."

"So it was you who made the decision not to use Ab on the Project after all, was it?" Rafe asked.

"Not by myself," said Martin quickly. "Actually, I was

part of a group we'd formed early, when we began to find out just what the power broadcasts were capable of doing. We were just hunting around in the dark, those days— that was five years ago—but one of the things we did was to put a few people like Ab into jobs where they could carry on research into the power-broadcast effects without attracting public attention. When you recommended Ab for the Project, though, that almost let the cat out of the bag. I was the one who rigged the decision not to use him —but it did give me a chance to have an interview with him. We hadn't met before. As a result, he and I, with Bill Forebringer, Pao, and a few others, were able to form a special secret clique inside the original group—a special clique that made it possible for us to set up quietly the machinery to get rid of Shaitan before he got rid of us."

"I thought," said Rafe, "I was the one who got rid of Shaitan for you?"

"You did. Of course," said Martin. "It's just that we were ready to move, ourselves, when you and Lucas and Gaby killed him—"

"I—" Gaby looked unhappy for a second; then her face smoothed out. "That's silly of me. I was going to say I hadn't anything to do with killing. But of course that doesn't matter. The main thing is that we're free of Shaitan now. And I'm no more or less guilty because he's dead than anyone else in the world."

She looked down at her brother.

"Am I, Ab?"

"No." Ab smiled up at her. "You're not. He was a creature—a creature slated for necessary extermination, so we can get on to making a new world for people."

"Only one new world?" asked Rafe.

Ab looked from Gaby back up at him.

"You hate to see the Far-Star Project set aside," Ab said. "I don't blame you. But part of the reason for having it was to solve a lot of the problems here on Earth— overpopulation, disease, mental distortions. All the effects of overcrowding. But now we'll be able to start solving problems like that directly with the side effects of the power broadcast, used therapeutically."

"That's what this group of yours was after?" asked Rafe.

"That, and a lot more," said Ab. His face lit up. "There's something else you came close to guessing when you talked to Gaby. There's an enabling effect as one of the side benefits of the power broadcasts. It's a different version of the effect that allows people like those thugs of Shaitan's to project themselves as what looks like two-dimensional shadows. But this effect simply gives the individual power over his own physical and mental processes. People are going to be able to cure themselves of anything, just by ordering their bodies to reject the disease. We'll be able to cancel out pain, or adapt ourselves to breathing under water. We'll be able to read pages at a glance and remember everything we read. Sleep when we want or go without sleep as long as we need to—anything!"

Ab bounced to his feet as if the energy in him had finally conquered the strength of will that had kept him sitting this long.

"And it's all waiting for us, now—now that Shaitan's out of the way!" He shoved his hand out toward Rafe. "Welcome to the group, Rafe. We've got a big job ahead of us, rebuilding the world together."

Rafe ignored the hand. He took two quick steps backward.

"No 'we' to it," he said. "There's a lot of truth to the story you're giving me. But you're a liar all the same, Ab. All of you here are lying to me, right at this moment. It's all right. I know you can't help it."

He continued to back. He was in the center of the open space of the long room now, turning as he went, watching every door and window.

"All right," he said, raising his voice. "Wherever you are—you ought to know by this time I'm not going to be stopped that easily. That explanation Ab just gave me's got holes in it you could march an army through—and I wouldn't doubt that's exactly what you've been planning to do. Let's get done with the fun and games. Don't you think it's about time you showed yourself?"

The sound of a whistle—something like the single bird-like shrilling of a bo'sun's pipe—fluted in a single note through the room. Abruptly, a power broadcast attempted to clamp a simple, but massive, paralyzing effect upon Rafe. Safe in the bastion of his under-mind, Rafe managed to deny its effect. But at the same time the air seemed to ripple, distort, and thicken about them all.

This time the distortion was worse than it had ever been

before. It hid both ends of the room from Rafe's view, and even the group around Ab and Gaby were distorted and obscured. At a shorter distance, however, Rafe saw panels open in the walls of the room, and three guard dogs came out to station themselves—one between him and the entrance, the other two between him and the opposite end of the room, where the thronelike chair was now hidden in the distortion.

The distortion cleared. The paralysis broadcast continued. The two guard dogs stood alertly on their feet, their eyes concentrating on Rafe alone. But beyond them the throne was now occupied.

The man sitting in it was gray-haired and dark-skinned, though his features were Caucasoid. He wore trousers and shirt made of black cloth thickly patterned with geometric figures in silver, and over both these garments, a long coat of unrelieved silver. There was nothing on his head. His gray hair was brushed straight back, and his face was unlined—but the way he sat suggested great age.

"Yes," said Rafe at the sight of him.

Rafe turned toward the group around Ab, who were now staring back at him with something like horror on their faces, as if they were watching a criminal being escorted to some ghastly but deserved punishment.

"Ab," said Rafe. "All the effects of broadcast power work only the conscious, intellectual centers of the mind. Behind and below that, if you can locate it, you'll find you've got a semi-instinctive level where thinking's still possible, in nonsymbolic terms. Try to reach back the way I have, and break loose of the broadcast effect holding you now."

Ab stared at him. Ab's lips slowly parted and his throat worked. He looked as if he was trying to talk, but no sound came out. His lips closed again.

"Keep trying," said Rafe.

He looked back at the man on the throne.

"The Old Man," Rafe said. "The real Old Man."

"Old enough." The voice of the man on the throne was husky and deep as if his throat had dried out long since. "But why do you fight me?"

"That's a foolish question," said Rafe. "I was born to fight you—or anyone like you. I'm the result of the human race's blind instinct to balance its parts. It couldn't be what I am without being anti-you."

"You pretend to believe in good and evil?" said the Old Man. "Why? You have to know they're both illusions. You can't be as capable as you are and cling to nursery tales."

"Nursery tales are true tales—if you understand them." Rafe took a short, casual step toward the other, and one of the two dogs nearest him stiffened and snarled slightly. Rafe stopped. "Good and evil are like parts in a play. You picked one part to play. That leaves me the other."

"It needn't be," said the man on the throne. "You're more like me than anyone else in the world. Why isolate yourself? Why destroy yourself?"

"Who's going to be destroyed remains to be seen," Rafe said. "Construction's what I'm after. I want people to keep on building. You want them to stop it."

There was a strange, throaty sound from Ab, as if a word was trying to tear itself loose from his vocal cords but lacked the strength.

"That's right, Ab," said Rafe, although he continued to keep his eyes on the man on the throne who sat utterly still, his hands folded in his lap. "Keep trying."

"You're my son, you know," said the Old Man to Rafe, ignoring the others, "my spiritual son, just as Shaitan was. Now you've killed your brother and you're the only one left. You can inherit the world from me when the time comes, if you won't fight me now."

"I don't want to inherit," Rafe said. "I want something to love. And I've chosen the human race for that—my race, I want this new power to go to them, to be used by them, for them, and for their future. So they'll survive and grow strong."

"Love," husked the Old Man. "That's also an illusion—like good and evil. There is no love. Any more than there's kindness or cruelty or achievement or failure. There's only survival, going on as far as possible until the stopping point. You're young. That's what makes you talk like this."

"And you're old—too old," said Rafe. "So old you'd make a world of slaves so that you could be the only one to go on living indefinitely—"

There was another faint sound from Ab.

"That's right, Ab," said Rafe, still with his eyes as unwaveringly fixed on the Old Man as the watchful eyes of the guard dogs were fixed on him, "that's what he wanted. That enabling effect you talked about, and I guessed at, is the sort of thing that could let a man mend his own body and guard it against the breakdown of old age. He's probably several hundred years old, our master here, but he still wants to keep on living. And he wants to keep on living as the absolute ruler and owner of the human race. Am I wrong, Thebom Shankar—if that's your name?"

"One of my names," said the Old Man. "But not the name for you to use. Out of all those in the world, I offer you now the chance to call me Father. Refuse the chance and I can't let you continue to exist. Decide. The time is short. Decide now."

"I've already decided," said Rafe. "I told you. The enabling effect will eliminate the need for the cryonic storage of cosmonauts on the long trips to the stars. Since men can live as long as they want, it won't matter how long the trip is—and even then, if time weighs too heavy on them, the cosmos can hibernate as long as they want and wake up when they're almost where they're going. This is what I want—not an endless life for just you, and for myself after you."

"You'll get neither, then." Thebom Shankar seemed to whisper, but his whisper filled the room as if he had shouted the words. "Only destruction. Have you forgotten the words of Zeus? I sang those words once, first under the name of Homer. Do you remember how Zeus tells the other gods to take one end of a chain while he takes the other, and they can see for themselves how his strength is still greater than all of theirs combined? For I'm also Zeus. My strength is greater than the strength of any number of sons—even if you had Shaitan, or a dozen Shaitans, alive again and joined with you against me. Acknowledge me or die. I'm lonely for companionship after all these years, or you'd never get this chance. Acknowledge me—"

Thebom Shankar stopped speaking. His eyes moved slightly to look from Rafe into the group around Ab. These stood or sat, apparently unmoved, but Rafe's eyes followed the direction of Shankar's gaze to the stiffly upright, seated figure of Forebringer. Forebringer's right hand had now moved from the arm of his chair and was halfway out of sight inside his plum-colored jacket. Looking closely, Rafe saw that the veins were standing out on the man's forehead and that the hand was slowly, slowly, as if against some great counterforce, inching its way into the jacket.

"Always"—Shankar's whisper once more filled the room—"there are little men who try the impossible. Watch and learn, my prospective son."

Shankar lifted his right hand slowly from his lap and pointed—not with his index but with his middle finger—at the UN Marshal.

"Willet Forebringer," he whispered. "In your desire to oppose me, to harm me, you offend me, and you are therefore of no more use to me upon this Earth. Willet Forebringer, I order you to die."

Something like the compulsion Shaitan had attempted to use upon Rafe as he held the huge man in a strangle hold washed faintly against Rafe's mind now. But it was the compulsion of a command, not to love, but to self-destruct, and it was aimed, not at Rafe, but at Forebringer. For a second or two more, Forebringer's hand continued to creep in under his jacket. Then it stopped. The stiffly upright body fell back a few inches against the back rest of the chair it sat in, and stayed there, staring now at the ceiling of the room. The halted hand fell from the jacket opening, onto the still knees, and a small handgun rolled from the lax fingers to the polished floor. Shankar's own hand dropped back down into his lap.

"So," said Shankar, bringing his eyes back to Rafe. "Every night now the whole world dreams under the power broadcast. And the carrier wave of that broadcast brings me the force, the charge, of all their released emotions. This comes to me, who gathers it in like a storage battery, to give me power of life and death as you've seen just now. Can you face a power like that, son-to-be? You know better than to think you can."

"Ab," said Rafe, his eyes still locked on Shankar's. "How're you doing, Ab? You know enough about the power broadcasts to believe you can break loose if someone like me can do it. I need help, Ab. You know what help."

"Son-to-be," said Shankar. "Now you've killed this other man. Even if you acknowledge me now, he'll have to die—"

"*Lucas!*"

The word tore itself suddenly from Ab's lips, as if shot forth by some inner explosion.

"Lucas!" Ab shouted again. "Now! *Now!*"

The three guard dogs were on their feet, their attention turned for the first time from Rafe to one of the two open windows. Shankar's hand, which he had half raised, stopped in mid-air. There was a rustle of plants from outside the window and a gray body shot over the sill of the window into the room. Lucas looked around at them all.

The guard dogs were bristling and growling. The one between Rafe and the entrance to the room was nearest to the window where Lucas had come in. It was crouched now, snarling, the hair bushed up on the back of its neck. Lucas's gaze swept down to Ab, moved across to Shankar.

Slowly, without a sound, the wolf walked toward the nearest dog, looking through and past it. The snarls of the dog mounted, clashing with the noise the other two were making. But none of the three moved from the spot where they were standing. Almost as if he did not hear or see them, Lucas moved on through the room, and as he got close to the nearest dog, the snarls of the animal lowered in volume. Its body crouched, lower and lower. As he reached it, finally, its belly was on the floor and its snarls had faded into whines. It rolled on its back before him, whimpering, reaching up at him with one paw.

Lucas stood over it for a second, pausing but still not looking down, making no sound himself. Then he moved on, past Rafe without looking at him, still at a walking pace, toward the other two dogs.

These doubled the sound of their snarling. They jerked about from one paw to the other, as if eager to move but held in their places by invisible leashes. Only as Lucas approached, they too lost their snarls in whines and gradually crouched before the wolf.

"Look at them, Shankar!" Ab's voice broke out, suddenly free, and loud in the room. "Did you think any training, or power broadcast, could make them face up to a wolf? The real controls are behind, as Rafe says—the old instincts stop them."

Lucas was past the last two dogs now. He paused, looking up at Shankar as he had looked up at Shaitan.

"Little men," said Shankar, "are always fools."

He lowered his half-raised hand to an arm of the throne

and touched it. A small aperture opened in the scrolled end of the throne arm, and a light winked momentarily.

There was a sharp, abruptly cutoff howl from Lucas. He leaped into the air, and a second later a smell of burnt fur spread through the room. Landing on the polished floor, Lucas struggled upright on shaky legs, and then—his eyes already glazing—turned and lurched to one side, throwing his dying body between Shankar and the chair where Gaby sat beside Ab.

"My . . ." rattled Lucas's voice. He tried to lift his head to Gaby's knee, but the reach was too far. "My Gab . . ."

His head dropped. He shuddered and lay still, dying but not yet dead.

For Rafe, the world broke open. For a last time, the old gut-twisting empathy woke in him—and joined his soul with Lucas's. Suddenly, he was the wolf and knew everything the wolf had loved and lost facing an enemy that had always been too well armed for the simple animal mind to defeat.

"*No,*" he said to Shankar, and it was as if he heard his own voice from a very great distance. Ab had fallen on his knees beside Lucas, and was fumbling with the side of Lucas's furry neck. Shankar still sat with his finger tips on the arm of his throne. "No," said Rafe. "Lucas isn't going to die. This time it's you who'll die—at my hands."

There was a terrible sorrow and a fury in him that had nothing to do with words. That which he felt could only be told by action. His eyes locked with Shankar's and there was no need for spoken words. Understanding flowed between the two of them—the understanding of two men who go aside together quietly, so that one may come back alone.

Lucas is the last, Rafe's understanding said to Shankar's. *The last of all those who came against you to be killed. No more living things will be killed by you . . .*

About the two of them, time and space were changing. Illusion or reality, it made no difference, for the only important realness now was the space that separated Rafe from Shankar. About them, the world shrank. The solar system, the universe, shrank until it was no more than a bubble from which the part where they two faced each other bulged upward, each smaller part bulging larger than the larger part to which it belonged—this world from the shrunken universe, this island from the tiny world, this building from the small island, this room, this little distance between Rafe and the man on the throne . . .

It was less than twenty feet, the distance that separated them. But it was also farther than twice around the universe. They stayed facing each other; and from room and island, world and universe, there flowed up to each of them, borne on a carrier wave of the broadcast power, that type of strength to which each was most kin, from all the other lives alive on Earth.

Like invisible rivers of fire, one bright, one dark—both sensed rather than seen—the strengths filled up in each of them. Rafe took a step toward the throne.

Shankar's fingers came down on the throne arm, and once more the light winked from the little aperture in the arm's end. But this time the laser beam that the light signaled had to reach twice around the universe to kill, and in the changed space between Rafe and Shankar it died harmlessly, barely inches from the throne.

Rafe took another step forward. The room darkened.

The wolf was only a beast, the understanding of Shankar said to Rafe, *and for his sake you've traded your chance of heaven for hell.*

He was one of all living things, answered Rafe, *and it was you who tried to trade his life for death.*

There was dark everywhere now except along the narrow path between them, where light still lingered.

Not even this matters, said Shankar.

All things always matter—this, most of all, said Rafe. He was walking against the power of Shankar now, which was trying to keep him from the throne, and it was like walking up a vertical slope. The last of the light went, and he was blind. But he could not be blocked off from the knowledge of where Shankar still waited, and he kept on moving toward the Old Man.

Son-that-will-never-be-now, said Shankar, *you should have believed me when I said your strength could never match mine. You're less than halfway here.*

I'm still coming, said Rafe.

The air went away from around him. There was nothing to breathe. All heat went, except that which he held inside him. He struggled on, feeling the cold and the airlessness plucking at his will.

You're half dead already, the understanding of Shankar reached him. *And I wait here, strong with centuries of dead men's strength. All that holds you up is the little good will of those alive today, of those who want the stars or mourn a dying wolf.*

If what I carry could be killed in the human race, answered Rafe, *both it and I would have died long since. Don't lie to me, true Father of Lies. The strength that comes to me is more unkillable, and older, than that which reaches you*

He was close now—he could feel the presence of Shankar, less than a fraction of a universe away.

Only a little farther, said Shankar. *You're almost to your death. Comfort yourself while you can with the dream that your strength is older and greater than mine. It and you will go down together. Heroes die, but evil never dies. Do you think Shaitan is dead because you helped kill him? Wait just a few years and there will be another just like him to skin small animals and hang them on upside-down crosses.*

Rafe made one last step and felt Shankar, at last, close enough to touch.

Now, said Shankar, *you are here. You've come this far to destroy me, but all you've done is brought yourself to me for your own destruction. Now, I point at you as I pointed at that other, and I say to you as I said to him: You have offended me, Rafael Harald, and I order you to die!*

Out of the darkness that still hid Shankar came the touch of something against Rafe's chest. It was like the end of an unyielding rod, with a cold so cold it burned against his heart clear through the heatlessness that had already almost frozen the life within him. He felt it now, burning the heart from him, and knew that he was dying. And still his hands had not closed on Shankar, sitting hidden before him in darkness.

I will, he thought with every particle of strength that remained in him. Thinking this, he flung himself forward on the rod of cold as a man might fling himself upon a naked sword in order to come to grips with his enemy.

His hands closed on darkness, and darkness came into his mind at last, taking it over utterly . . .

17

And so Rafe Harold died.

But he was not allowed to remain dead. A time came when sight and hearing returned to him. He recognized that he lay on a white bed in a white room and that Gaby and Ab and others came to see him from time to time.

Then one day, without warning, a gray, shaggy head shoved itself over the edge of the bed, took his wrist gently in jaws that could have crushed it like a chicken wing, and whined. Then words came back to him at last.

"Lucas?" he said.

Someone touched something at the foot of the bed in which he lay, and the upper third of the bed tilted, raising him so that he saw not only Lucas, but Gaby and Ab and another man in a business suit and with a stethoscope hanging around his neck.

"Yes," said Lucas. "I'm here."

"You ought to know it'd be Lucas," Ab said to Rafe. "You were the one who wouldn't let him die."

"I?" said Rafe. "How did you know that?"

"I told them," said Lucas.

"As soon as he could talk again, he told us," said Gaby. "And now, finally, you've started to talk, too." Her voice trembled a little on the last words.

Rafe slowly shook his head. There was a bitter hollowness in him that he had to disappoint them.

"It's over," he said. "I died. Shankar killed me."

"Come on, now!" said Ab. "We know better than that. Your heart's as steady as a metronome." He grinned at Rafe. "We can't help it if you've been too lazy to get out of bed."

Rafe did not smile back.

"Shankar," he said. "Where is he?"

Ab sobered.

156

"Cremated," Ab answered. "We thought we might as well play safe."

"Play safe?" Rafe stared at Gaby's brother. "You mean he's dead, too?"

"You killed him," said Lucas, "and made me live."

"I?" Rafe sat gazing from Lucas to the rest of them. "I couldn't have. He killed me first."

He saw them watching him with eyes that did not believe him.

"I don't even remember touching Shankar," said Rafe. "How could I have killed him?"

"You touched him, all right," said Ab. "You took forty years, it seemed, to walk from where you were up to where he sat. But when you got there, you fell on top of him, and both of you fell out of the throne onto the floor. All of a sudden, then, we could all move, and when we got to you and Shankar, you had your hands on his neck and he was dead."

"Hands?" said Rafe. He looked down at his hands lying on the white bedspread. They were thinner than he ever remembered seeing them, fragile looking.

"If he killed you first," said Ab, "then you broke his neck after you were dead. And that's not possible, even for someone like you."

"Isn't it?" said Rafe. And then, even through the lightlessness of his mind, a bitter humor took him. He chuckled, still looking at his hands. "Reflexes!" he said. "The fastest man in the world. Just fast enough, when the time came, to kill someone after I'd been killed myself."

"Only you hadn't been—and you aren't," said Ab. "Let's drop all this talk about being dead. You send shivers down my spine. You're sitting here talking to us, aren't you?"

"It makes no difference," said Rafe. He knew as he said it that they would never understand. He looked at all of them, but mostly at Gaby, with a terrible longing. "I'll be going away shortly."

"Doctor," said Ab to the man with the stethoscope, "will you please tell him he's alive?"

"I give you my word, Mr. Harald," said the man with the stethoscope, looking straight at Rafe. "Your body's perfectly healthy and operating normally in every way."

"I believe you," said Rafe. "But it doesn't make any

difference. What happened, happened. I lost my fight with Shankar. He killed me first, and I died."

"Yes," said the voice of Lucas unexpectedly. "It's true; Rafe died. For me." The fierce jaws gently massaged Rafe's wrist. "I'm here. Always. I'll go with you, Rafe."

"No!" exploded Gaby. "Neither one of you is going anywhere! Rafe, you're staying with me. It's all nonsense and it doesn't matter—" She swung fiercely around to confront Ab and the doctor. "Do you understand? It *doesn't matter*—alive or dead or whatever!"

She turned back to Rafe.

"And *you* understand!" she said. "You'll stay. Both of you'll stay where I can watch you from now on!"

Rafe looked back up at her sadly.

"It'll never work," he said.

But strangely, even as he said it, he felt the first, faint stirrings of a doubt in himself about that. It was true he had died—*died* in a sense that they who had never experienced it could never understand. But it might not have to be true that death was the end of everything, after all.

He had been changed, but was it irrevocably for the worse? His empathy, his reflexes, were not gone—though they were temporarily in abeyance, they would come back —but somehow the barrier they had always erected between him and the rest of mankind was no longer there. He felt his feelings washing freely between himself and these others around his bed. He could *feel* for Gaby without *becoming* her. Surely that sort of change was for the better.

It had been Shankar's philosophy, not his, that death was a final end. And he had fought and killed Shankar to prove that philosophy wrong. The laws of the universe, any universe, could not be unchanging if that universe was to survive. They must change every day to adapt to new circumstances. Lucas lived. And it might just be that in his own case there was a new life waiting for him—a life among people, rather than apart and above them. It might be that Gaby had life in her enough for both herself and him, until he could win his way back among the living once again.

It just might be. It might be, after all . . .

Numerical Checklist of DAW BOOKS
NEVER BEFORE IN PAPERBACK

All DAW books are 95¢ (plus 15¢ postage & handling if by mail)

DAW BOOKS are represented by the publishers of Signet and Mentor Books, THE NEW AMERICAN LIBRARY, INC.

THE NEW AMERICAN LIBRARY, INC.,
P.O. Box 999, Bergenfield, New Jersey 07621

Please send me the DAW BOOKS I have checked above. I am enclosing
$_____(check or money order—no currency or C.O.D.'s).
Please include the list price plus 15¢ a copy to cover mailing costs.

Name_____

Address_____

City_____State_____Zip_____
Please allow at least 3 weeks for delivery